DISNEY
DISENCHANTED

Adapted by Steve Behling
Teleplay by Brigitte Hales
Story by Bill Kelly and
J. David Stem & David N. Weiss

Based on Disney's *Disenchanted*

DISNEP PRESS
LOS ANGELES · NEW YORK

Printed in the United States of America
First Hardcover Edition, October 2022
1 3 5 7 9 10 8 6 4 2
FAC-004510-22252

Library of Congress Control Number: 2021949329
ISBN 978-1-368-08268-6

Visit disneybooks.com

~ PROLOGUE ~

Once upon a time, in a magical fairy-tale land called Andalasia, there lived a chipmunk named Pip. He was a small woodland creature, not so magical compared with some of the other citizens of Andalasia, but what Pip lacked in size and magical abilities, he more than made up for with his enormous heart. Also his loudness. He was a very loud chipmunk.

But one night he was quieter than usual.

It was bedtime for his two children, Kip and Nip. He was reading them a story, hoping they would soon settle down to sleep.

"Once upon a time, in a magical kingdom called Andalasia, a baby was found in the forest," Pip began. "With no mother or father to speak of, the baby was raised by the animals, who loved her as one of their own."

The children sat and listened, enraptured.

"And her name was Giselle," Pip continued. "Giselle grew into a beautiful young lady with a loving heart and a secret desire."

Pip told of how Giselle yearned to share true love's kiss with a handsome prince.

"Until one day she won the love of the bravest prince, and it seemed like she might finally have a happily-ever-after of her very own."

Of course Pip was speaking of Edward, a very brave man who had a way with a song—and a sword.

"And then—" Pip started.

"Giselle was banished by the Evil Queen to a dark and scary place called New York City," Nip interrupted.

Pip held the storybook as Kip and Nip restlessly wriggled about.

"There she met some disgusting, but helpful, animals," Kip said playfully.

Nip then turned to the wall of their home and made shadow puppets of cockroaches just like the ones that helped Giselle in New York City.

Pip sat back as his children continued.

"She also met Robert!" Kip said. "Who had a daughter and dreamy eyes, so they fell in love!"

Pip remembered everything like it had happened only yesterday: Giselle, banished to New York City, encountering Robert and his young daughter, Morgan. The two of them taking in Giselle and showing her kindness.

Then, with great excitement, Kip told how Giselle had become cursed and had been kissed by Robert, and how together they had faced an evil queen who had transformed into a dragon!

And Nip just had to point out that they had all lived happily ever after. He made a pair of shadow puppets dance on the wall to illustrate his point.

Pip blinked. Of course the kids' version of the story glossed over some of the details. For example, there was Nancy, a friend of Robert's and Morgan's, who had ended up meeting Edward. They fell in love and had their *own* happily-ever-after in Andalasia.

Then Pip closed the storybook and said, "So ya heard that one."

"Read it again!" Nip begged.

"Dad, do you think when Giselle moved to the kingdom of New York that she forgot all about Andalasia?" Kip asked.

Before Pip could answer, Nip chimed in. "Course she didn't, Kip! She had her Memory Tree!"

"Nip's right," Pip said. "Everyone from our land's got a magical Memory Tree, no matter where they end up. And that means no Andalasian can ever forget what's most important. 'Cept for that one time she and I forgot everything that was most important."

"What?" Kip exclaimed.

"When was that?" Nip asked, astonished.

With a deep sigh, Pip got up and walked to the bookcase.

"Okay, there might be a little more to Giselle's story," Pip admitted as he pulled a dusty book from the shelf. "Not exactly proud of my part in this, but if you get in bed, I'll tell it to ya."

As Pip sat down in his chair, he opened the book. The two boys couldn't wait for the story to begin.

"It all starts pretty much where the last part ended," Pip said. "In the kingdom of New York *after* happily ever after."

"After?" Kip interrupted. "But there's no after happily ever after."

"Yeah," Nip agreed. "You just get married, then nothin' ever happens to you again."

Pip grinned. "Not in *that* world. Over there, things

never *stop* happenin'. For Giselle, a few years went by, Morgan sprouted up, and soon . . ."

The children looked in wonder at the book, where they saw Giselle and Robert holding a baby! And there was Morgan as a teenager.

"Robert and Giselle had a baby, a beautiful girl named Sofia," Pip said. "And for one moment, Giselle truly had it all. And *that's* when things began to change."

Pip turned the page. Kip and Nip saw an illustration of Giselle and her family. They were all getting in one another's way in their small apartment.

"First their castle in the sky felt like it shrunk two sizes," Pip explained. "Then . . ."

As Pip turned the page once more, the children saw Giselle in the dress shop she owned. On the opposite page, there was Robert in his office, working late. Both Giselle and Robert were buried in paperwork.

"Robert and Giselle got so busy at work it was often *midnight* before their days were even done," Pip said.

Once more the page turned, revealing Morgan in her bed with a phone in her hand.

"But hardest of all was Morgan," Pip said. "She became what that world calls a teenager, and it felt to

Giselle like she'd gone to a faraway place where she could never go."

As Pip flipped the page, Kip and Nip saw Giselle standing in the doorway of Morgan's room. Morgan stared at her phone, not even noticing Giselle.

The page turned again, and they saw Giselle walking with Robert and Morgan and pushing baby Sofia in a stroller along the crowded streets of New York City.

"Giselle started wondering if maybe the kingdom of New York *wasn't* her happily-ever-after at all. And *that's* when she saw a sign."

Pip turned another page, showing Giselle as she looked at a sign featuring a beautiful small town and the words MONROEVILLE—YOUR FAIRY TALE STARTS *HERE*.

"And suddenly, they knew what they needed to do," Pip said. "They had to go after their happiness, no matter where it went. And so . . ."

The next illustration showed three large moving trucks parked outside Robert's apartment building.

"They packed up and set out . . ." Pip said.

~ CHAPTER ONE ~

Outside Robert's apartment building, the door of a moving truck slammed shut. Wide-eyed and hopeful, Giselle looked at the truck as her long red hair flowed down around her shoulders.

Every inch the princess, Giselle smiled as the movers hurried by, filling up the remaining trucks with possessions from their apartment. She saw Robert, multitasking as he almost always did, phone pressed to his ear as he pushed past the movers in the doorway. He held Sofia in his other arm as the baby cried.

When Giselle first met Robert, he was a divorce attorney working at a big New York City law firm. He was strictly a "just the facts" kind of person. Robert knew the law inside and out, backward and forward.

But once he met Giselle, he was forced to set logic aside and embrace the more wondrous, almost magical aspects of life. And then, of course, there was the actual magic, and he had embraced that, too.

Handing Sofia to Giselle, Robert ruffled his brown hair and said into the phone, "Yep, have the case file right here."

"You promised no work today," Giselle reminded Robert.

He covered the phone and said, "Goldman divorce is almost done. Five minutes, I promise."

Then Robert ducked back inside the apartment building as Morgan came out, carrying multiple bags of belongings. She unenthusiastically tossed them into their car.

"That's all of it," Morgan said, sounding defeated. "I'm gonna sit in the car now and say goodbye to ever having friends again."

Giselle looked at Morgan sympathetically. "I know. It's hard to leave good friends," she said.

Then Giselle glanced at a nearby tree, where several pigeons and even some mice were perched, watching her every move. The birds cooed, and the mice squeaked with sadness.

"But now we get to make *lots* of new friends," Giselle said hopefully. "Monroeville is *wonderful*."

As Giselle continued, she was surprised that Morgan spoke in unison with her: "It's the closest thing to Andalasia I've ever seen. Our house is like a castle, and you have your own room."

"Yeah. You've told me a *million* times," Morgan said.

"Well, happy things are worth repeating," Giselle noted, "and *singing* when you can. Don't forget the trees! Some of my fondest memories are growing up in a tree."

Morgan stopped herself from rolling her eyes.

"Yep, a *magic* tree in *Magic* Land," Morgan said dryly. "I'm sure it's exactly like that."

Giselle paused for a moment, then said, "Is that—"

"Sarcasm?" Morgan replied. "Yes. Yes, it is."

Giselle didn't understand sarcasm. Why would anyone say something but mean something else? It didn't make sense.

Her thoughts were interrupted by the crashing of a moving box marked FRAGILE. The mover looked sheepish as Sofia cried loudly, startled by the sound.

Holding one last pile, Robert rushed out of the apartment building.

"All right, that's it," said Robert, out of breath. "Let's hit the road. Who's ready?"

"I'm not," Morgan answered, "which you both know and don't care about."

Robert suggested they stop for ice cream first. He hoped his peace offering would work.

Morgan thought for a second. "Fine," she said. "Double fudge, and you're on." With a last look at the apartment, Morgan got into the car.

Robert grinned as he looked back at the apartment building where he had spent many happy years with Morgan and Giselle. Behind him, the moving trucks drove away. Giselle secured Sofia in her car seat.

"Let the adventure begin," Robert said.

As they headed off to Monroeville, Giselle looked out the car window. She waved goodbye to the pigeons and the mice. They waved back.

Morgan was on her phone immediately, trying not to look out the windows at the city—the *home*—she was leaving behind. Next to her, Sofia sat in her car seat, happily throwing toys.

Then Giselle began to sing a cheerful song all about their new lives in their new suburban town. Giselle sang about Monroeville as if it was a dreamland, like Andalasia.

Giselle's song continued as big buildings began to disappear, replaced by the tree-lined highway that led to Monroeville.

As they drove down the rural highway, there was a loud thunk. Suddenly, the car lurched to one side as a tire blew out. Robert pulled the car to the side of the road.

"Even the car doesn't wanna leave the city," Morgan groaned.

A quick phone call and a little while later, help arrived. The flat tire was replaced while Morgan held Sofia and watched. Then she handed Sofia off to Giselle. The baby promptly spat up on Giselle.

Then the replacement tire went *pop*! It rapidly deflated.

Morgan shook her head as Robert asked for one more tire.

∽◇∽

Giselle had changed into a worn, comfy sweatshirt with WORLD'S GREATEST MOM emblazoned on it. She held Sofia while the tire was replaced once again.

Robert emerged from behind the car, dirty but grinning.

"And we're off," he said. *"Again."*

As the car traveled down the country road, they approached a sign that read WELCOME TO MONROEVILLE YOUR FAIRY TALE STARTS HERE!

Driving into town, the family looked out the car windows at the quaint main street, full of adorable shops. A clock tower sounded the hour.

At last, the car pulled up outside their new home. Morgan looked at the house and saw the turret. That indeed made the house appear somewhat like a fairy-tale castle, except the turret was in serious need of repair. In fact, the whole *house* looked like it was in serious need of repair.

When they exited the car, Morgan saw a plumber fixing a pipe, a painter putting a fresh coat of paint on the house, and gardeners trimming hedges. The movers had already arrived and were unloading boxes.

Robert walked up to the house with Morgan.

"So this is the 'castle' you've been raving about," Morgan said.

"They're a little behind schedule," Robert said, trying to sound positive. "You just need some vision."

"Or *no* vision at all," Morgan added.

Giselle walked up behind them with Sofia in her arms.

"Okay, so we have a little surprise for you," Giselle said with excitement.

"For me?" Morgan asked.

Giselle took her by the hand and practically dragged Morgan into the house.

The inside of the house was more disastrous than the outside. There were workers everywhere—painting walls, sanding floors, and fixing electrical wires.

"Now close your eyes," Giselle said to Morgan.

But before she could, Morgan heard a loud crash. A woman sanding the floor had fallen through the rotting floorboards.

"I'm all right!" the woman shouted as she struggled to pull herself out of the hole. "I think."

"Just step around that first," Giselle said awkwardly.

Morgan stepped around the hole and closed her eyes. She headed upstairs, with Robert leading the way. Giselle glided up the steps behind them, with Sofia cooing in her arms.

When they reached the top of the stairs, Giselle walked Morgan to a doorway.

"Okay, open your eyes," Giselle said.

When Morgan opened them, she couldn't believe what she saw. Inside the doorway was a perfect full-on princess room with a large canopy bed and a flowery mirror on one wall.

Stepping inside, Morgan tried to find something to say.

"I got a little carried away, I know," Giselle admitted. "And you can change all of it. I just wanted you to have a real room when you got here. I made them promise it would be done."

"Only thing that mattered to her," Robert added.

Then he pointed toward a wall. Morgan saw a collage of her artwork. In the center was a tree made of construction paper. The tree was covered in pictures of her dad, Giselle, and her younger self. Written on top of the tree, in her own handwriting, were the words MORGAN'S MEMORY TREE.

"It's very pretty, Mom," Morgan said, softening.

"Really?" Giselle replied. "I'm so glad you like it. Pretty soon the whole place will feel like home. You'll see!"

Giselle smiled at Robert, who mouthed, *Thank you.*

Then Morgan flipped a light switch on the wall. Without warning, the electrical wiring in the wall sparked. Electricity raced across the wires in the wall and along the ceiling, then down another wall, going through boxes of Morgan's clothes, until there was a small explosion at the base of the wall.

"Oh!" Giselle exclaimed as everyone stared in disbelief.

"Those were *all* of my clothes," Morgan said.

"Hello!" came a voice from downstairs. "Hello! Helloooo!"

Robert looked at Giselle, confused. "Do we know someone?" he asked.

"No, but now we can!" Giselle said.

They headed back downstairs, where they saw three women. One of the women stood in front of the other two, who were holding large baskets. All three were trying to avoid the plaster falling around them.

"Hope you don't mind," the woman standing in front of the others said. "Door was open. Giselle and Robert, right? And Morgan. Oh, and little Sofia."

"Why, yes!" Giselle said, impressed. "How did you know?"

Holding out her hand, the woman said, "Malvina *Monroe*. I would've sold you this house, but I deal in slightly more *upscale* homes. I was so glad someone finally saw the charm of this place."

Then Malvina became quite intense as she said, "Rosaleen and Ruby. *Let's welcome them.*"

Immediately, Rosaleen and Ruby handed the baskets to Robert and Morgan.

"She made it all herself," Rosaleen pointed out.

"Even the baskets!" Ruby noted.

"I weave," Malvina said with pride.

"Well, that's very nice of you," Giselle said.

"And a little weird," Morgan jabbed.

"Morgan, why don't we take these to the kitchen?" Robert said as he ushered her out of the room. "Great to meet you."

When Morgan and Robert were gone, Malvina observed Giselle's sweatshirt with a disdainful eye.

"I see you're also a bit crafty," Malvina said. "It's . . . a look."

"Oh," Giselle said, looking down at her sweatshirt. "Morgan made this when she was younger."

"That age was wonderful, wasn't it?" Malvina replied. "I have a teenager, too. Always pouting, but he's the apple of my eye."

"*Everyone's* eye," Rosaleen chimed in.

"Even people with *no* eyes!" Ruby added.

Malvina shrugged. "Now, if you all need anything, I'm your gal. Probably know this town better than anyone. I like to be involved in this and that."

"It's true," Rosaleen agreed.

"She's like a queen around this place," Ruby added.

"Then I'm doubly honored," Giselle said. "I think every land should have a queen."

That night, Morgan lay on the floor of Giselle and Robert's bedroom in a sleeping bag. Robert gently placed Sofia in her bassinet, then got into bed.

"Listen to that," Robert said. "So much better than Fifth Avenue."

"But just as loud," Morgan observed.

"The crickets are *very* happy we're here," Giselle said as she entered the room. "They've composed this entire song for us. We should build them a playground. I bet they don't have one of those."

Morgan gave Giselle a quizzical look. "Do crickets need that kind of thing?"

"Oh, everyone needs a playground," Giselle said. "I'll chat with them about it tomorrow. Right after we get your room all fixed up."

"Great," Morgan replied, "because you both promised me I'd have more room in this house, and this feels like less."

"Nothing a little paint can't fix," Robert said, trying to raise his daughter's spirits. "Tomorrow's a new day, Morgan."

"And it's going to be a *great* one," Giselle added.

~ CHAPTER TWO ~

Whesn the alarm sounded, Morgan shot up from the floor. It was still dark outside. She heard her dad slam his hand on the alarm clock. The sound woke up Sofia, who began to cry. Then Giselle and Robert, wiping the sleep from their eyes, got out of bed.

"*Why* is the alarm going off?" Morgan complained. "It's still *yesterday* outside."

"I'm a commuter now," Robert said. "Up with the sun."

Morgan covered her face with a pillow.

In the kitchen a little while later, the morning rush began. Giselle darted back and forth, trying to make breakfast, but nothing seemed to be working. The oven wouldn't turn on, the toaster was smoking, and even the coffee maker sputtered concerningly.

Through it all, Sofia cried from her high chair.

A bluebird landed on the kitchen windowsill and chirped.

"Oh, uh, yes, it's a *lovely* morning," Giselle said, trying to sound cheery.

Robert rushed into the kitchen. He quickly kissed Sofia. Giselle turned, awaiting her kiss, but it never came. Robert blazed right past her, grabbing a mug.

"*So* late," he said, failing to notice Giselle's disappointed look. "Don't quite have this down yet."

Morgan rushed in a moment later in wrinkled clothes. "It's a miracle!" she announced. "One shirt surviv—"

Right then, Robert reached for the coffeepot, lifted the handle, and accidentally spilled coffee. Most of it landed on Morgan, absolutely drenching her shirt.

"I'm so sorry," Robert said. "Are you okay?"

"Yeah," said Morgan, crestfallen. "But that was my *only* outfit."

Before he could say anything, Robert was distracted by a loud crash outside. Giselle scooped up Sofia from her high chair. They ran out of the kitchen into the backyard.

There they saw a well gushing water into the air. The water turned into golden balls of glowing light, creating a shimmering mist. And through that mist appeared a handsome man with sparkling blue eyes. Accompanying him was a woman with dark, wavy hair and a warm smile. It was Edward and Nancy!

The workers were shocked. They carefully peered inside the well as the water disappeared.

Giselle squealed with delight as Morgan and Robert followed her.

"What are you two doing here?" Giselle asked, greeting Nancy with a big hug.

"We *had* to open a portal to your new place!" Nancy explained.

"Meant to do it sooner, but Snow White and her brood showed up," Edward added.

"Hate it when that happens." Morgan chuckled.

"Oh, look who's gotten sassy," Nancy observed. She wrapped an arm around Morgan warmly.

Meanwhile, Robert and Edward awkwardly looked at each other.

"Robert," Edward said, grasping for something to say. "Congratulations on the increasing size of your progeny." Then he looked at the house, still in shambles. "So, are you poor now?"

"Edward . . ." Nancy interjected.

"No, we're not poor," Robert answered, a little insulted.

"It's what they call a fixer-upper," Giselle said.

"Ah, I see," Edward replied. "Well, I'm sure it will look much better once your peasants have dug out your moat."

"And on that note . . . I'm off," Robert said as he walked away.

"Come on, I'll show you the house," Giselle said, excited to have company.

"It's more the *idea* of a house," Morgan offered.

Nancy laughed at Morgan's joke, and they headed inside. Edward lingered for a moment.

"Robert!" Edward shouted, running over to him. "It appears you've forgotten your sword."

"Don't have a sword, Edward," Robert said.

"Oh, I just assumed now that you're a country squire, you would have more need of a sword," Edward mused.

"Nope. Still a lawyer."

"In that small box in the sky?" Edward asked.

"An office building," Robert said. "Yes. It's not usually a place for swords."

"How tragic," Edward noted. "I can only imagine how desperate you must be to truly *do* something."

Again, Robert felt a little insulted. "I do plenty, Edward."

"Of course," Edward said. "I understand. A brave front is required to face a life as barren as this." After a brief pause, Edward said, "Perhaps this will help."

In a fluid motion, Edward quickly removed his sword. Robert ducked, narrowly avoiding having his head chopped clean off.

"This sword and I have slayed many a beast together and seen magnificent adventures, which have tested both body and spirit," Edward explained, oblivious to the fact that he had almost accidentally decapitated Robert. Then, handing the sword to Robert, he said, "May it do the same for you."

Edward intensely patted Robert on the shoulder. Then he headed back to the house, leaving Robert holding a sword in one hand and his briefcase in the other.

"That never gets easier," Robert sighed as he headed to the train station.

Edward entered the house and reunited with the others. A worker did a double take at Edward in his royal Andalasian garb. Edward noticed the worker's overalls and returned the look.

"So, there's actually another reason we're here,"

Nancy admitted as she glanced at Sofia. "We missed her birthday last month."

"Sudden uprising of forest gnomes," Edward explained.

"But we had to make sure the goddaughter of the king and queen of Andalasia got one of these," Nancy said, presenting an ornately carved box. She opened it, revealing a sparkling wand inside, along with a scroll.

Interested in all the sparkling, Sofia grabbed the wand.

"An Andalasian Wishing Wand!" Giselle gasped.

"A *what* wand?" Morgan asked.

"A *wishing* wand," Giselle said. "I always heard about them, but I've never actually seen one."

"Well, when your godparents are the king and queen, they have to bring something extra special," Edward explained.

Then Edward and Nancy formally presented the box. They sang about the wand, about using it for good intentions, and about following the rules, of course.

"Does anyone in Andalasia ever just say stuff?" Morgan asked.

"Not if they can help it!" Giselle answered brightly.

Edward and Nancy continued their song, revealing that the wand could be wielded only by a *true* descendant of Andalasia. And that if there were any problems or additional questions, they could ask the scroll.

When the song ended, Giselle carefully took the wand from her daughter. "How about that? You're a *true* Andalasian."

Morgan felt a sharp pang of jealousy.

"Well, unless you have a wand in there for a *fake* Andalasian, I have to get dressed," Morgan said. Then, before Giselle could say anything, she added, "Yes. I'll look in your closet. I'm sure there are lots of fun options in there."

Morgan turned and clomped up the stairs.

"Sometimes she says one thing but means the opposite," Giselle said, a little hurt. "I can never tell."

Edward and Nancy looked at each other, noting Giselle's distress.

But Giselle had already brushed it off. She walked into the kitchen, placing the sparkling wooden box with the wand inside on the windowsill.

"Do you ever find it easier to live in Andalasia?" Giselle asked.

"I wouldn't say 'easier,'" Nancy said. "We've got dragons and ogre rebellions, and every so often a magic curse just falls over the whole place."

"Yes, but you can slay a dragon," Giselle retorted. "And magic curses are almost always reversed, eventually. The problems in this world are much different."

Nancy nodded. She had lived most of her life in that world and understood where Giselle was coming from.

But Edward did not.

"If this world isn't to your liking," he said, "then you should change it."

"It's not that simple, Edward," Nancy protested.

"Hogwashery," Edward announced. "If anyone can make something out of *this*"—he gestured at everything around him—"it's our Giselle."

"Maybe you're right," Giselle replied.

"Okay, but in case it's a little more difficult than that, just remember," Nancy said, "Andalasia is always there when you need it."

~~~

At the train station, Robert boarded the morning commuter train without incident. With a paper bag in one hand and coffee in the other (and his briefcase and sword under an arm), he settled into a window seat.

While other passengers boarded, he tried to pull his bagel out from its bag with one hand.

It wasn't going very well.

A businesswoman sitting next to him said, "You should tell 'em no bag."

Robert saw the woman holding a bagel wrapped in paper. Then a bunch of commuters held up their bagels, all wrapped the same way.

No one had a paper bag.

"Got it," Robert said. "Still getting the hang of commuting life. Used to be a ten-minute walk."

A disgruntled businessman stared at Robert and said, "Don't worry. You've got plenty of time."

"You're gonna ride this train over and over. And over and over," the businesswoman said. "And then ya die!"

"That's kind of cynical, isn't it?" Robert replied.

"Just reality, man," a tired-looking businessman said.

Everyone around Robert nodded in agreement. Then he looked at his sad bagel bag and felt his spirits deflating.

∽ CHAPTER THREE ∽

Giselle and Morgan, with Sofia in the stroller, stood in the bustling courtyard of Morgan's new high school. Morgan watched groups of teenagers heading toward the entrance. They were all talking and laughing like they'd been friends for life, which they probably had.

But not Morgan.

All *her* lifelong friends were back in New York City.

As they walked farther into the courtyard, Morgan felt that she stuck out like a sore thumb in the pastel shirt and busy floral skirt she had borrowed from Giselle.

"I cannot pull off this many flowers," she said grumpily.

"Don't be silly," Giselle said encouragingly. "You look beautiful. You want me to wait?"

"Do you see any other parents here?" Morgan shot back.

Giselle was about to answer when suddenly she gasped at the sight of a huge bake sale table set up across the courtyard. There was a big sign that read TYSON MONROE FOR MONROE-FEST PRINCE! Beneath it was a picture of a teenager, presumably Tyson Monroe.

Behind the table stood Malvina, along with Ruby and Rosaleen. Anxious-looking parents stopped by, dropping off baked goods to be sold.

"She really *is* involved," Giselle noted.

A nervous couple handed over a tray of brownies. Rosaleen picked one up and then measured it.

That's right.

She *measured* it.

"Perfect squares. Congrats!" Rosaleen said.

The couple sighed with relief as their brownies were deemed worthy of being placed on the bake sale table.

Then a rumpled-looking dad handed Ruby a plate of poorly iced cupcakes.

Ruby dumped them into the trash.

"Fondant," Ruby said icily. "Google it next time, or it's off with your head."

The dejected dad walked away. Giselle and Morgan

approached Malvina as she organized several perfectly iced cupcakes.

"You are *very* talented with baked goods," Giselle said.

"Oh, it's just a little fundraiser," Malvina said with a trace of false modesty.

Morgan looked at the cupcakes, then glanced at the banner, reading aloud. "'For . . . Monroe-Fest.' What's that?"

"It's our biggest festival of the year," Rosaleen explained.

"With candy apples! Malvina's specialty," Ruby bragged.

"I'm told they're to die for," Malvina said with a smirk. "And there's lots of other food, almost as good. Some games. A fun little vote for prince and princess."

"Tyson's won prince three years in a row," Rosaleen stated.

"Even when he broke both his legs, he *still* won," Ruby said.

"I promise it's not rigged," Malvina joked. "The whole weekend is really a celebration of everything that makes Monroeville so magical," she continued. "It probably sounds quaint to city people."

"Not at all!" Giselle said sincerely. "I *love* festivals! We had them all the time where I'm from. They were often interrupted by evil forces of some kind, but when they weren't, they really did bring people together. I'd love to help if you need it."

Giselle enthusiastically placed a dollar into a donation jar.

"You should take her up on that," Morgan said. "She once made a forest out of six thousand M&M's, then had it delivered to my class by pigeon. No one beats her with this kind of stuff."

"Is that so?" Malvina asked.

The conversation was interrupted by the first bell.

"Well," Morgan said, "time for my execution."

Giselle placed her hands on Morgan's arms, giving her daughter a comforting squeeze.

"Stop it. You'll be *great*," Giselle said.

Morgan looked into Giselle's eyes, and for a few seconds, she believed her. Then she took a deep breath and headed into the crowd of students.

"Just believe in yourself!" Giselle yelled over the noise of the crowd.

Morgan paused, not believing that Giselle would embarrass her like that in front of everyone . . . and yet believing it entirely. Some of the students chuckled. It gave Morgan a sinking feeling in her stomach that she didn't like.

Malvina noticed some of the parents and students looking at Giselle almost as if they were mesmerized.

"If you have the time, Giselle, I'd love to buy you some coffee to hear more about this M&M masterpiece, and whatever else there is to know about our newest Monrovians," Malvina said.

"Oh, I'd love that!" Giselle replied without hesitation.

Malvina forced a smile.

When Morgan turned a corner down a crowded hall, she slammed into three girls staring at their phones. Morgan's books were knocked to the floor. Without missing a beat, the girls kept walking.

"Livin' the full cliché here," Morgan said to herself.

Kneeling down, she started picking up her books. Then a hand reached out to her. Looking up, Morgan saw it belonged to Tyson—the boy from the banner. He gathered the rest of Morgan's books.

"They probably have an urgent selfie to post," Tyson joked.

"Well, it won't post itself," Morgan said.

Tyson grinned at her. "You're the new girl from New York."

"Morgan," she said, introducing herself. "And you're Tyson, from cupcakes."

"Ah," Tyson said knowingly. "You met my mother. I try to ignore whatever she's doing. She gets kinda intense."

"Imagine if she was made of magic," Morgan said.

"Oh, no," Tyson said with a shudder. "That would be bad for everyone."

Just then, the second bell rang as someone called out from across the hall.

"Tyson, come on!"

Tyson looked at a group of impatient teenagers.

He handed the books to Morgan. "Well, I'm sorry you had to move here, 'cause nothing ever happens in this town. If I were you, I'd get back to a real city as soon as possible."

"Wish I could," Morgan replied.

She watched as Tyson smiled, then headed off. Morgan realized she felt a little better.

When she turned, some extremely fashionable girls were staring at her, perplexed by Morgan's outfit.

Morgan sighed, the good feeling gone.

"I hate this town," she muttered under her breath as she headed to class.

~~~

"I just love this little town!" Giselle said, happily walking down the main street, pushing Sofia in her stroller. Malvina walked beside them as they passed by the quaint little shops. All around them, workers were hanging banners in preparation for Monroe-Fest.

"It's busy, but not too busy, and your woodland creatures are very clean," Giselle noted. "It's a perfect place."

Malvina whipped out a pair of small pruning shears and quickly cut off a dead flower protruding from a bush.

"Well, I've had to create a dozen committees to get it like this," she said. "And there's always more to do. Everyone thinks all this just magically appears, but it's actually a lot of work. Sometimes I wish I could *make* everything exactly the way I want it to be."

"Oh, you *can*," Giselle said, her voice full of positivity. "You just have to believe that you can. Like one day, when we're settled, I'm going to open my shop right here. I can already see it."

"So you run a business, too," Malvina said. "I guess we're both trying to have it all."

Giselle looked confused. "Isn't everyone?"

Malvina grinned as they entered a cute café with couches and mirrored walls. A small tinny bell at the door announced their presence.

A quietly intense man standing behind the counter slid a cup of coffee toward Malvina.

"Extra-large cappuccino with five shots," the man said. Then he turned his attention to Giselle. "And lemme see—herbal tea. *Hibiscus.*"

"That's right," Giselle said, surprised.

"Edgar knows everything going on in Monroeville," Malvina said conspiratorially. "When you're ready to open that shop, he has all the gossip."

"Caffeinated people love to talk," Edgar explained. Then he lowered his voice as he got in close to Malvina. "Yoga House broke up with Vegan-ville this morning. It was *not* zen."

"Bet there's no om for that," Malvina said with a chuckle as she looked at Giselle. "You might have a spot sooner than you think."

Malvina took her coffee, leading Giselle to a throne-like chair. Giselle noticed there was a sign on the chair that read RESERVED.

Rosaleen and Ruby were already there, on either side of the chair.

"You two move very quickly," Giselle noted.

"Shortcuts," Rosaleen offered.

"And running," Ruby said, a little out of breath as she pulled a leaf from her hair. Malvina took down the RESERVED sign and sat.

"As you can see, Giselle, our town is really just one big *family*," Malvina said. "And like any family, everyone has their *place in it*. Once you've found where you fit, Monroeville can be . . . whatever you wish."

Giselle smiled in response, clearly not receiving the unspoken threat in Malvina's words.

"I think you're right," Giselle replied.

When Morgan arrived home from school, she wasn't surprised to find Giselle in the living room, leaning over what looked like a miniature playground composed of toothpicks and bottle caps. A sign on top of the whole setting read WELCOME, CRICKETS!

Sofia cooed happily in her playpen.

"Morgan, how did it go?" Giselle asked.

"It was fine," Morgan answered, even though she certainly didn't sound fine.

She headed straight for the stairs.

Giselle gave Sofia a concerned look.

In her bedroom, Morgan sorted through her clothes, tossing all the burned items into a large garbage bag. Since pretty much everything was burned, pretty much everything went into the bag.

It wasn't long before she heard a soft knock on her door. Then it opened, and in came Giselle.

"Does this mean it didn't go well?" Giselle inquired.

"Well, no one talked to me all day, so I got a lot of me time," Morgan said. "That was nice." Then, before Giselle could respond, Morgan added, "And yes, that was sarcasm. My day *sucked*."

Stuffing a burned T-shirt into the garbage bag, Morgan sighed. Giselle was about to say something else when she noticed a small triangle of green paper sticking out of the bag.

Pulling it out, Giselle saw that it was the Memory Tree that had been on Morgan's wall. The pictures on it were intact. They were only a little burned on the corners by the previous day's electrical problem.

"Oh, this is nothing a little glitter couldn't fix," Giselle said.

"What's the point?" Morgan shrugged. "It's old anyway."

"The *point* is that it's a memory," Giselle said. "And as we say in Andalasia—"

"Memories are the most powerful magic of all," Morgan said, finishing her sentence. "I know. Not sure it works the same way here."

Giselle looked at the floor and sighed. She was tired of fighting with her daughter.

"Morgan, I know you didn't want to come here," Giselle said. "But if you give it a chance, it *will* get better."

"Or maybe it won't," Morgan shot back, "and I should go back to school in New York. I can take the train with Dad."

"It's only been a day," Giselle pointed out. Then, without realizing it, she repeated Malvina's earlier words. "We just have to find where you fit in. *And we will.*"

"*We* won't do anything," Morgan insisted. "If I have to do this, I'll do it myself. Okay? I don't need any bluebirds involved."

"Yes," Giselle said. "Of course. You can do it yourself."

"But if I give it a try and it still doesn't work, I'm going back," Morgan said pointedly.

Then she dropped the full garbage bag into Giselle's hands.

Giselle left Morgan's bedroom, closed the door, and headed to the kitchen. She dropped the garbage bag on the floor and placed the Memory Tree on a side table.

She sighed. Then she saw a flyer for Monroe-Fest.

This gave Giselle an idea. . . .

∼∼∼

The following morning, Morgan rose groggily, then headed downstairs.

She was surprised that Giselle wasn't there to greet her.

"Hello?" Morgan called out.

There was no response. Her dad had left for work, but Giselle should still be home.

When Morgan entered the kitchen, she had her answer. The room was littered with art supplies. On the table was a plate of carefully cut toast, along with a note that read

MEET YOU AT SCHOOL!

I HAVE A WONDERFUL IDEA!

Morgan grimaced.

"Oh, this can't be good," she said.

When Morgan arrived at school, she moved through the crowd of students in her slightly singed clothes.

Unlike before, however, everyone seemed to notice her. They gave her coy smiles that made Morgan feel uncomfortable. She rounded a corner and saw an enormous sign that read VOTE MORGAN FOR MONROE-FEST PRINCESS!

But that wasn't all.

There was also a huge image of Morgan, perfectly drawn on a shower curtain.

Morgan cringed. Beneath the banner, Giselle stood at a table with an impressive cupcake display.

Students and parents swarmed the table, hoping to get their hands on one of the scrumptious-looking treats.

"Vote for Morgan!" Giselle said. "She's new here and she's *lovely*."

"This tastes like *magic*," someone said.

"Actually, in this land you call it chocolate," Giselle replied.

Morgan was beside herself.

"*What* are you doing?" she said to Giselle as she approached the table.

"Well, I started thinking," Giselle replied. "We had festivals like this in Andalasia, and *everyone* knew the festival prince and princess. Now everyone will know you, too."

A vein in Morgan's temple began to throb. "I told you I'd figure it out," she said, her voice rising. "Why couldn't you let me do that?"

Giselle looked around. She noticed people staring at them. "I was just trying to help," Giselle explained.

"Yeah, well, good job," Morgan said sarcastically.

As she stormed off into the crowd of parents and students, Tyson arrived. "Morgan, wait," he said.

But Morgan kept walking.

Giselle was about to go after her daughter when Malvina arrived with Rosaleen and Ruby.

"I'm sorry, Giselle," Malvina began, "you can't have a table on school property without being an official member of a committee."

"Oh," Giselle said, distracted. "I didn't know. . . ."

"Well, I suppose now you do," Malvina said tersely. Then she snapped her fingers and said, "Ladies . . ."

At once, Rosaleen began taking down Giselle's marvelous display. Ruby, however, just stared at the table.

"These cupcakes are incredible," Ruby said.

"Ruby," Rosaleen scolded. "Serious face."

Realizing her mistake, Ruby put on a serious face and joined Rosaleen in taking down the display.

But Giselle hardly cared about that now. Her heart was breaking for Morgan.

Giselle sat on the living room couch as the clock struck ten. She held Morgan's Memory Tree and stared at it with sadness in her eyes.

Robert paced back and forth, hanging up his phone. "She must have turned off her phone," he said angrily. "I don't care if her entire room is ash. She's never leaving it again."

Giselle was silent. She kept running her fingers over the pictures on the Memory Tree of her and Morgan when she was little. They were hugging each other. They were happy.

"You remember when we made this?" Giselle asked.

"I dunno, maybe?" Robert said, distracted.

"She used to beg me for stories from Andalasia every night," Giselle said. "And her favorite ones were always about the magical Memory Trees. She loved them so much."

Robert sat down next to Giselle. "She's just growing up," he said calmly.

"But *nothing* is like it was anymore," Giselle said. "We don't talk, and when we do, I never say the right thing. I thought at the very least we might make some new memories here. I mean, some good ones."

"We will," Robert said, trying to comfort his wife. "But you have to give it a second. Things don't magically change overnight."

"Don't *you* want it to change, too? You don't seem much happier."

"That's not true," Robert said, taken aback.

"Isn't it?" Giselle asked. "When was the last time you were truly happy, Robert?"

Robert hesitated. "It's not that I'm unhappy," he finally answered. "Sometimes I just wonder if all I'll ever do is ride a train over and over until I die."

"Why would you do that?" Giselle said, horrified.

Robert realized that out of context, what he said didn't make a lot of sense. But before he could explain it to Giselle, a key turned in the lock of the front door. Morgan walked inside. She didn't look the least bit sorry for her late arrival.

"Where have you been?" Robert demanded.

"I went to New York," Morgan replied flatly.

"New York?" Robert said, astonished.

"By yourself?" Giselle asked.

"I've been riding the subway alone since I was thirteen," Morgan pointed out.

"I can't believe you would do this," Robert said. "What were you thinking?"

"I don't know, Dad," Morgan replied, her voice dripping with sarcasm. "Maybe that you should have left me where I belong."

"Morgan, you belong *here*," Giselle said, trying to comfort her daughter.

Morgan wasn't having it.

"No, I don't, and now I never will," she said. "I know you wanna live in some perfect fairyland, but we don't. We live *here*, in this stupid town, *and I hate it*."

Giselle was nearly in tears.

"Hey, you can be mad at me all you want, but don't talk to your mother like that," Robert said.

"My mother?" Morgan protested. "She's not my *mother*. She's my *step*mother."

Giselle was stunned. Morgan glared at her.

"And that's all she'll ever be."

Giselle was speechless.

"Morgan!" Robert shouted as his daughter stormed up the stairs. She slammed her bedroom door.

"Stepmother," Giselle repeated, almost in a whisper. Did Morgan really think she was a wicked stepmother?

Giselle headed for the door.

"Giselle, she didn't mean it," Robert said.

Giselle walked outside, the door slamming behind her. She breathed in the late-evening air and felt the darkness all around her. The urge to sing came over her. So, like the true Andalasian she was, Giselle put her feelings into song.

She sat down on the edge of the well. As she stared inside, Andalasia appeared like a reflection on the water.

In the watery image, Giselle saw Pip the chipmunk, who had heard his friend's mournful song. He couldn't just sit around. If he could help Giselle, he would.

So Pip popped up out of the well, crossing through the barrier between Andalasia and this world once again.

"Hello, old friend," Giselle said with a weak smile.

Then Giselle noticed something sitting on the kitchen windowsill.

"The Wand of Wishes," Giselle said softly.

She ran inside the kitchen, opened the box, and took the wand out.

"That's it," she said.

Pip chased after her, squeaking in his chipmunk voice. He tried to talk Giselle out of whatever it was she had planned.

"Maybe I shouldn't," Giselle replied. "But what choice do I have? If I want happiness here, I have to *make* things the way I want them to be."

Then Giselle headed back outside with the wand in her hand.

Once more she sang, as she prepared to make her wish.

She clutched the wand and closed her eyes tightly. Giselle knew what she wanted: for her and her family to have a fairy-tale life.

And with that, the wish was made.

A faint shimmering sparkle fell over Giselle and Pip.

Giselle opened her eyes expectantly.

Everything was exactly the same.

Giselle slumped, disappointed.

"Guess it didn't work," she said.

Pip felt bad for his friend, but he was also relieved. If the spell *had* worked, what problems might it have caused?

"Oh, well," Giselle said. "Tomorrow is another day. Why don't you sleep over? We have some very comfortable twigs."

That sounded wonderful to Pip. He hopped onto Giselle's shoulder, and they went inside.

If they had lingered for another minute, they would have seen vines and flowers crawling up and around the sides of the well.

The clock in town chimed midnight.

It was like something from a fairy tale.

~ CHAPTER FOUR ~

When Giselle awoke the next morning, she noticed a warm light shining in through the bedroom window. It was almost like a magical glow.

Two bluebirds landed on the windowsill, chirping happily. Giselle usually greeted any bird with a brilliant smile. But that morning, she couldn't muster one.

"It's not a very good morning at all, I'm afraid," Giselle said sadly.

The bluebirds looked at Giselle for a moment. And then, in unison, they said, "Well, then you just have to *make* it a good morning."

Giselle wasn't yet fully awake, so she didn't notice anything out of the ordinary.

"You know, you're absolutely right, Mr. and Mrs. Bluebird," Giselle said. "I should—"

Then it hit her. That sounded a lot like Malvina's words from the café. She gave the bluebirds a surprised look, but they flew away.

Giselle got dressed, went to Sofia's room, and carried her daughter downstairs.

Along the way, she thought of Morgan and the awful confrontation they'd had the previous night. Giselle wanted to show Morgan how much she cared about her. Luckily, she knew exactly what to do.

"Okay, so we'll make her favorite breakfast with whipped cream on *everything*," Giselle said to Sofia. "What do you think?"

Sofia giggled.

"You're filled with giggles today!" Giselle said.

Still in her nightgown and robe, Giselle walked into the kitchen and gasped. All the appliances in the room had come to life! The toaster was busy making toast. The coffeepot brewed while making a happy bubbling sound. A spatula tossed a pancake onto a plate, and a whisk was beating a bowl of eggs—all by itself.

Not only that, but everything was singing a song about making breakfast.

Then Morgan entered the kitchen. She was dressed a little drably, but she glowed with happiness.

"Beautiful morning, isn't it?" Morgan said. Then she began to sing a song about how she enjoyed doing chores.

Giselle was shocked. This was a *very* different Morgan from the one who had run off to New York City the previous day!

Then Robert, wearing what could only be described as regal attire, walked into the kitchen.

"Giselle!" Robert called out. "You're even more beautiful than you were yesterday."

He gave her a kiss.

Now it was Robert's turn to sing—about going on a quest.

With a broad grin, Robert took Giselle by the waist and dipped her. He kissed his wife again, and they began to dance around the kitchen. Morgan danced, too, with a broom.

"Well, I'm off," Robert said once their dance ended.

"And I'm off, too," Morgan added. She took Sofia from Giselle and said, "But not without my little helper. Chores are an adventure all their own. That's what I say."

Robert, Morgan, and Sofia left the kitchen as Pip

scampered down the stairs. The chipmunk rubbed his sleepy eyes as he entered the kitchen.

"Those twigs were murder on my sciatica," Pip said. Then his eyes popped wide open. "Hey, I'm talkin'! Wait, *how* am I talkin'?"

Giselle looked at the Wand of Wishes on the windowsill. A feeling of gratitude came over her. The wand sparkled.

Unnoticed by Giselle, the sparkling wand had caught Sofia's interest prior to Sofia's departure from the kitchen.

"Pip! The wish I made last night," Giselle said with excitement, "for a fairy-tale life? I think it came true."

"What do ya mean?" Pip asked, incredulous.

Giselle gazed out the window. "Look," she said in awe. "We're in a fairy tale."

She raced to the front door and stepped outside. Pip followed her.

Indeed, the whole world seemed to have been transformed overnight. The average suburban front yard had been replaced with a remarkable kaleidoscope of color. There was a horse-drawn carriage in the driveway, where the family car had been parked. The turret, badly in need of repairs the day before, was a glimmering tower.

Even the workers had transformed into fairy-tale versions of themselves. The painter now had a long beard, almost like Rip van Winkle. The three gardeners resembled magical fairies. And the plumber was dressed in a manner that suggested the Pied Piper.

"Jumpin' jelly sticks!" Pip hollered. "We got magicked! Oh, geez. Do I got all my parts?" The chipmunk quickly checked himself, making sure he had his arms, legs, and tail.

"I hate magic," Pip groaned.

Giselle had a reply, but she didn't say it.

Instead, she sang.

Her song was about the new world around them and how they most *certainly* would enjoy their happily-ever-after again.

~~~~

Giselle, still wearing her robe, raced down Main Street, her marvelous mood unshakable. She noticed the town sign now read WELCOME TO MONROLASIA— YOUR FAIRY TALE IS HERE!

The same buildings were all there, but they seemed more whimsical than they had the day before.

All the townspeople, dressed in fairy-tale-style clothes, gathered along the street to join Giselle in song and dance.

Giselle's heart swelled with joy as Morgan arrived, pushing Sofia in her stroller. Giselle glimpsed something sparkling in her baby daughter's hand.

When the song ended, a large carriage rolled down the street.

"It's the queen!" Morgan gasped.

"The *who*?" Giselle asked.

A valet hurried to the side of the carriage and opened the door with a flourish. Out stepped Malvina, dressed in the finest royal wardrobe with a dark twist.

She exuded evil queen vibes.

"Oh!" Giselle said, innocently looking at Malvina. "Monrolasia has a queen. Looks like everyone got their wish."

Then Ruby and Rosaleen exited the carriage, mimicking Malvina's elegant moves. Giselle noticed Ruby's large red earrings, which perfectly framed her face. They were fluffing the train of the queen's dress when they accidentally dropped it into a puddle of mud.

Malvina didn't seem to notice. Her attention was focused on a dead flower in a planter. This time, instead of using a pair of pruning shears, Malvina simply waved her hand. The flower magically bloomed a deep bloodred color.

"And she's a *magic* queen!" Giselle said. "Those are always fun."

"Uh, Giselle?" Pip said, picking up on Malvina's ominous vibes.

Before he could say anything else, the crowd bowed before Malvina. Pip had to dodge knees. Then he tripped over his feet, falling into a grate with a splash.

Malvina noticed Giselle, still wearing a nightgown and robe, and walked over to her.

"Giselle, how *lovely* to see you," Malvina said in the most insincere manner possible.

"It *really* is," Ruby agreed.

"Not so much for me," Rosaleen whined.

"Out doing some last-minute shopping for tonight, are we?" Malvina inquired.

"What's tonight?" Giselle asked. Then she hastily added, *"Your Majesty."*

"For the festival, milady!" a villager shouted.

"Of Monrolasia, milady?" a woman reminded Giselle.

Looking up, Giselle saw the banners announcing Monroe-Fest still hanging. Except it was now called the Festival of Monrolasia!

"The festival!" Giselle said, remembering. "It's still happening?"

"Why wouldn't it?" Malvina said. "There's no power on Earth that could stop it. It's *my* little gift to *my* people."

"Of course, *Your Majesty*," Giselle said, slightly amused.

Malvina sensed that something was going on. Whatever it was, she would get to the bottom of it. She looked at Morgan, with Sofia in her arms. And then something in the baby's hand caught Malvina's eye.

It was a wand.

A sparkly wand.

"That's an interesting trinket," Malvina said.

The queen slowly walked over to Sofia and reached for the wand, but Giselle glided between them, blocking the queen's path. She didn't want Malvina holding the wand. Who knew what might happen?

"It's nothing," Giselle said. "Just a silly toy."

"A toy?" Malvina echoed. "Is it, now?" Then she leaned toward Sofia and said slowly, "May I hold it, dear?"

At once, there came a loud chime from the clock tower. While it had been impressive the day before, Giselle noticed that the clock tower was now truly majestic, rising into the sky, looking like one of the beautiful ornate towers from Andalasia.

The clock struck twelve. As it did, Giselle's eyelids fluttered ever so slightly. She felt the tiniest shudder.

In that instant, something about Giselle's entire demeanor shifted. While she had been all warmth, Giselle now seemed a bit icy and a little wicked.

"Why don't you just focus on your little *party*?" Giselle said to Malvina in a somewhat haughty tone. "After all, baked goods are what you do best. *Your Majesty.*"

Then she took the wand from Sofia and tucked it into her nightgown. It was very un-Giselle-like.

A second later, Giselle shuddered again, and her warmth returned.

"That was wicked," Rosaleen muttered.

"The wickedest," Ruby confirmed.

Giselle looked around, suddenly wanting to be anywhere but where she was.

"You know what? I just realized," Giselle said to Morgan, "it's your first-ever fairy-tale party. You'll need a dress! We'd better get right on that. See you tonight, Your Majesty!"

Before Malvina could reply, Giselle and Morgan hurried away. The queen watched them leave, her mind racing.

"Do *we* need new dresses?" Ruby asked.

"We got some, remember?" Rosaleen answered. "To match with Her Majesty's."

"But I look terrible in purple," Ruby grumbled. "What about fuchsia? I look great in fuchsia."

"Stop saying 'fuchsia,'" Rosaleen fired back.

"Something is going on with her," Malvina said, interrupting them. "And I want to know *what*."

~~~~

Robert strode with purpose through Monrolasia, enjoying the warm sun on his face.

This is a good day for a quest, he thought, feeling the hilt of the sword hanging from his belt. He was determined to seize any opportunity for adventure.

Then, finally, Robert saw it: a man walking his dog.

Trotting over to them, Robert said, "Excuse me, good sir. Have you or your miniature beast seen any adventure about?"

The man scratched his head, thinking. "Like what kinda adventure?" he asked.

"I'm not exactly sure," Robert said. "Perhaps a darkness on the land requiring extraordinary bravery to overcome it?"

The man looked up at the clear blue sky.

"No clouds today," he replied.

"A helpless villager trapped in a tower?" Robert asked.

"Nope," the man answered.

Robert sighcd. "Disappointing," he said.

"Have you tried the Enchanted Woods?" the man

asked. "Feels like there's always something going on in there."

That instantly perked Robert up. "Of course! The Woods of Enchantment!"

Then Robert raced off to the woods—for *adventure*!

A little bell dinged as Malvina opened the door and entered the café with Rosaleen and Ruby directly behind her. Inside the café, courtiers sat atop mushroom seats, feasting on a variety of treats. On Malvina's arrival, they all stood.

"Everyone out," Malvina ordered.

The courtiers immediately cleared out of the café.

Malvina walked to her throne-like chair. She glared at a mirror on the wall.

"Mirror, mirror, on the wall," Malvina began, "who's the most *powerful* of them all?"

Malvina awaited the answer. When it didn't come, she grew annoyed.

"Mirror?" Malvina snarled. *"Mirror."*

At last, a face appeared in the mirror. It was Edgar, who only the previous day had run the coffee shop. But he was now the Magic Mirror!

"Did you not hear the question?" Malvina asked.

"I did, Your Majesty," Edgar answered. "But I'd rather not end up shattered on the floor if I can help it."

"Tell me who it is," Malvina demanded.

Edgar sighed. His image in the mirror slowly faded. It was replaced by an image of Giselle.

She stood in a store, looking through dresses on a rack.

Malvina sneered.

"But it's *always* you," Rosaleen said in disbelief.

"He must not understand," Ruby said. Then, loudly, right into the mirror, she said, "We said '*most powerful.*' Not 'the prettiest.'"

That made Malvina fume.

"I heard you just fine," Edgar said. "My apologies, Your Majesty. I don't know what's happened."

"*I* do," Malvina said. "It's that wand she was being all coy about. It was dripping in magic. Even a fool could see that."

"That wand was magic?" Ruby asked innocently.

"So obvious," Rosaleen said, as if she had known all along that the wand was magic, which, of course, she hadn't.

"Actually, Your Majesty, now that you mention it, I did hear something about a wand this morning," Edgar said. "I assumed it was idle gossip, since the only one allowed to have power in this town is *you.*"

"You're right," Malvina agreed. "I *am*." Then she snapped her fingers and barked, "You two, get it for me."

"You mean steal it?" Ruby said.

"Yes, Your Majesty," Rosaleen added.

Rosaleen pulled Ruby out of the café as Malvina waved her hand over the mirror. An image of Giselle, shopping for dresses, without a care in the world, appeared once more.

"Oh, Giselle," Malvina mused. "What have you done?"

In her robe, Giselle pushed aside one dress on the rack to look at another, still feeling odd from what had happened in the town square. Why had she spoken to Queen Malvina like that? It certainly wasn't like Giselle to speak to someone with wickedness.

"Dresses have really changed since I was almost a princess," she said.

Then she saw a glass slipper and shouted, "Oh!"

Giselle picked it up and started to try it on when suddenly something came over her. "Not on my watch, dearie," she sneered.

"If it fits, it's yours," a saleswoman said, watching Giselle try on the slipper.

Giselle shuddered as the saleswoman wandered to her side.

"House policy," the saleswoman explained.

Giselle appeared shaken as she put the slipper down, eyeing it warily.

"Not exactly what we're looking for," she said.

"H-how do I look?"

Giselle turned toward the voice to see Morgan in a stunning Cinderella dress. The gown was a shimmering sea of sparkling blue and white.

"Oh, Morgan," Giselle said. "You look wonderful. What do *you* think?"

Morgan looked at her reflection in the mirror.

"It's beautiful," she said with a smile.

Giselle smiled back at her daughter. For the first time in a very long while, the two shared a bonding moment.

"Then we'll take it," Giselle said.

"I'm sure it's very expensive," Morgan said, hesitant. "You don't need to do this."

"Of course I do," Giselle insisted. "I've always dreamed of sharing a night like this with you, and it's going to be *perfect*. Now we just need some shoes."

Giselle and the saleswoman were heading toward the shoe rack when Morgan saw something out the store window.

It was Tyson, dressed in princely garb and riding on horseback. He looked directly at Morgan and mouthed the word *market*.

Blushing, Morgan headed back toward the dressing room.

"So, Ms. Giselle, we must find a dress for you, too," the saleswoman said.

"Oh, no, thank you," Giselle said. "This dress will do just fine."

"Nonsense," the saleswoman stated. Then she pulled out a rack of extremely sparkly dresses.

"*These* are one of a kind," the saleswoman explained. "Hand-dipped in *actual* fairy dust. You will twinkle like a star."

Giselle admired the dresses.

"It's a very aggressive twinkle," Giselle said politely, "but I don't really need—"

Her words were cut off by the chimes sounding the hour from the clock tower. It was as if the sound stunned her.

Walking to the window, Giselle stared at the tower and shuddered. A coldness swept through her. It was the same sensation she had felt an hour prior, when the clock struck twelve.

"Ms. Giselle?" the saleswoman asked.

Giselle swiveled around with a look of superiority. She glared at the saleswoman.

"Is everything okay?" the saleswoman asked.

Giselle strutted toward the mirror, looking at herself, as if for the first time. It was clear from the expression on her face that she was in love with the way she looked. Vanity had consumed her.

"I was just thinking . . . I really *do* have the figure for fashion," Giselle said.

"The finest hourglass would shatter with envy," the saleswoman said eagerly.

"And for a figure so fine, only the best will do," Giselle said. "Don't you think?"

"No other wares can compare. With ten percent off for a beauty like you," the saleswoman replied.

That was music to Giselle's ears. She glanced at the rack of expensive dresses and said, "Let's try 'em all."

~ CHAPTER FIVE ~

Robert again felt the stirring call to adventure when he came upon a tavern. Once inside, Robert noticed that the tavern was packed with patrons. He saw a prince, a huntsman, a warrior, and more than a blacksmith or two. If Robert hadn't been so consumed by his newfound thirst for thrilling quests, perhaps he would have recognized them as the commuters from the train the day before.

They were all drinking out of mugs. They all appeared to be miserable.

But not Robert.

"Good morning, fellow travelers!" he enthusiastically announced. And then, in song, he stated his intention of finding a quest to test his mettle.

"Great," said a warrior, rolling her eyes. "Another one."

"Grab a mug, buddy," said a grumpy prince.

A woman handed a mug to Robert, then walked away.

"What? No!" he said. He couldn't waste the day socializing indoors. "Out there is the adventure we seek," he proclaimed.

"Used to be," a tired huntsman said, correcting him.

"Now it's just walkin' through woods, over and over. And over and over, then ya die!" the warrior complained.

"But I feel this compulsion to seize the day," Robert admitted.

"I did, too," the warrior said. "Once upon a time."

"We all did," the huntsman said.

"But adventure is what we are made for," Robert said, trying to rally the crowd to his side. "Surely we will find it."

"That's what I used to think, too," the huntsman said.

Everyone in the tavern seemed to agree that it was more difficult now for adventurers.

They sang about their problems, and then they danced. Oh, how they danced!

The crowd was still quite full of energy and enthusiasm but had nowhere to channel it now—or so they thought.

Robert joined in the song and told everyone that he wanted to seize the opportunity to show the world that heroes still exist.

They all thought he was overly optimistic, but Robert remained undeterred. He was just beginning his journey. How could it end so suddenly?

Somehow, Robert's zest and zeal rubbed off on the patrons, and they started to think that maybe—just maybe—if Robert succeeded in his quest for heroic adventure, there could be hope for other heroes.

"Then I'm off!" Robert shouted above the din as he charged toward the tavern door. Everyone cheered, raising their flagons.

Notably, they did not follow him.

The corner of Giselle's mouth curled into a cruel-looking smile as she gazed at the many, many bags from the dress store resting on a chaise in her home.

Then Giselle looked at Morgan, who held Sofia.

"I'd say we did *very* well," Giselle offered.

"A little *too* well," Morgan rebutted.

Morgan set Sofia in her bassinet near the window. Giselle pulled the Wand of Wishes from her dress and placed it on a side table.

"Blech!" Pip said, walking into the room. "What's that smell?"

He was dripping wet, his fur matted. Pip looked like a hot mess.

"Oh, hey, it's me. Know why? I fell into a *gutter*. And look!" Pip said, gesturing to himself.

"That's odd," Giselle said. "You're usually so nimble."

Pip looked at his reflection in a lamp, inspecting his eyes and sticking out his tongue to see if anything was amiss.

Meanwhile, outside Giselle's home, Ruby and Rosaleen tiptoed up to the window. When they peered inside, Pip caught their reflection on the lamp and whirled around. Ruby and Rosaleen ducked out of sight. Confused, Pip shook his head.

"I'm tellin' ya, something ain't right with me," Pip said. Then he noticed all the shopping bags on the chaise. "Geez, ya buy the whole town?"

"Well, it's not *all* for me," Giselle said in a voice that suggested it was mostly for her. "Imagine our Morgan, the belle of the ball . . ."

Shyly, Morgan cast her eyes downward as Giselle picked up one of the garment bags.

"In *this*," Giselle said.

Ruby and Rosaleen stood up and looked through the window once more.

Then, with dramatic flair, Giselle unzipped the bag to reveal a dress made of tattered rags.

"Hmm," Morgan said. "Looks different in this light."

Giselle stared at the dress with a look of shock.

At that moment, Ruby snuck her hand through the window, moving slowly toward the wand. Baby Sofia was the only one who noticed.

"What happened?" Giselle said, sounding surprised. "This thing's been torn to shreds. It's barely fit for a maid."

"Not exactly how I woulda put it," Pip said, confused by Giselle's out-of-character behavior.

With all the stealth she could manage, Ruby reached out to grab the wand. But Sofia knocked it on the ground first. Thwarted by the baby, Ruby scowled.

"I'll just do some mending," Morgan said.

Ruby refused to give up. If Malvina wanted the wand, Ruby would get it for her! She clambered atop Rosaleen, balancing on her head. She leaned even deeper inside the window and managed to grab the wand. She was just about to leave when Sofia grabbed on to Ruby's hair—and pulled. Hard.

Ruby silently screamed, wondering how a baby could pull so hard.

"No one is mending anything," Giselle said briskly. "I will march right back to that store and demand an explanation. I just don't understand why anyone would want a dress made of rags."

With a hard yank, Ruby freed herself from Sofia's impossibly strong grip, and she disappeared back through the window. In the commotion, she failed to notice that one of her ruby earrings had fallen to the floor.

Morgan turned and picked up Sofia. "Well, I'm going to put Sofia down for a nap. Then I'm off to market so I'll have plenty of time to get ready for the festival. I have a feeling this is going to be a night I'll remember forever."

"Mmm-hmm," Giselle said, clearly not paying attention to a word Morgan was saying.

Just as Morgan was about to leave the room, she looked back at Giselle.

"Thank you for everything, *Stepmother*," she said.

She exited as Giselle snapped back to her old self.

Gazing at the dress made of rags, she said in a horrified tone, "*Stepmother.* Oh, no."

"What?" Pip said.

Giselle raced to the mirror and took a long look at herself. Her worst fears were confirmed.

"Look at my hair!" she gasped. "It's so high. And this

dress. It's so low! And I *almost* sang in a minor key this morning. I *never* sing in a minor key."

Then Giselle grabbed the dress made of rags and showed it to Pip.

"And of course I'd want this to look like rags. People like me always do!" Giselle said.

"People like *who*?" Pip asked, genuinely confused. "What are you talkin' about?"

"Pip, my wish is suddenly turning me into a . . ."

"A what?" Pip asked.

"Into a . . . wicked stepmother!" Giselle gasped, the words nearly stuck in her throat.

"What? Come on," Pip said. But then he looked at Giselle, and her very un-Giselle-like hairdo, and the dress, too.

"Actually, yeah, I totally see it," Pip finally admitted.

"Oh, Pip," Giselle said, with panic in her voice, "I can't be a stepmother in a fairy tale. It'll ruin everything with Morgan. I'll make her scrub the floors, and hate any boy she likes, and . . . Oh, no! The *attic*!"

With that realization, Giselle raced upstairs to the attic. Pip followed closely behind. When she burst through the door, a complete and utter mess was waiting. The attic was covered in a layer of thick dust, with cobwebs in every corner. On the floor was a lone, sad-looking mattress. There were only a few personal possessions, just enough to suggest that this was someone's bedroom.

"Who lives in this rathole?" Pip wondered.

"Morgan does!" Giselle said. "Stepdaughters always live in attics or dungeons. Oh, Pip, do you know what this means? I'm the villain of Monrolasia!"

"Well, you're not the *only* villain," Pip pointed out, as if that made anything better.

"Don't be silly," Giselle said. "There's only ever *one* villain, not counting minions, or pets, or villains you don't know are villains until it's too late."

Pip squinted and said, "Well, Monrolasia's different, 'cause there's *you* and then there's that evil queen ya made."

"Who, Malvina?" Giselle asked innocently. "Oh, she's not evil."

"Maybe not in that other world," Pip said. "But did you see that outfit?"

Giselle gasped. "Oh, you're right!" she said. "I created an evil queen! They're never up to anything good!"

"No, they ain't," Pip replied. "So you'd better do somethin' quick, before she hatches a plan to kill us all—"

Suddenly, Pip stopped talking.

"What's wrong?" Giselle asked.

"I don't feel so—" Pip started.

Then he grabbed his stomach and fell to his knees.

"Pip!" Giselle shouted.

The chipmunk began to twist and turn. Then his body began to change. His tail grew longer as his body enlarged. His ears turned pointy. Falling to the floor, Pip saw that he was now on all fours, panting.

"What just happened to me?" Pip asked.

Giselle stared at her changed friend and said, "Pip, wicked stepmothers don't have chipmunks as friends. They have—"

"*Cats!*" Pip shouted. "And evil ones!"

Looking at himself, Pip was stunned to find that he was now, in fact, a cat.

"I can't be an evil cat," Pip said. "They *eat* chipmunks! Oh, I'm gonna be sick."

Buoyed by the hearty singing in the tavern, Robert walked through the fairy-tale-looking forest full of flowers in bloom. He noticed butterflies gently fluttering past. But the placid scene was broken by a scream.

Robert drew his sword as he rushed to a small clearing. There he saw fire shooting from the mouth of a cave.

He was elated.

A group of villagers stood nearby and milled about. Running to the group, Robert noticed that the villagers looked tired—all of them except for a little boy.

"Are you a dragon slayer?" the little boy asked.

"I am," Robert confirmed. "And never fear, I shall slay the beast!"

"I wouldn't if I were you," one of the villagers said weakly. "It's very large."

"And cranky," another villager added.

"A cranky dragon is just what I'm looking for," Robert vowed. "Won't be a minute."

Taking a deep breath, Robert charged into the cave with his trusted sword leading the way.

Then he was thrown *out* of the cave.

He hit the ground hard. The villagers winced at Robert's predicament.

"Yes," Robert said, brushing himself off as he got to his feet. "Quite cranky."

Robert once more raced toward the cave, this time a little less enthusiastically.

Fire shot from the cave entrance, and Robert ran back.

"That is very hot," Robert admitted.

"You're on fire, sir," one of the villagers whispered, pointing at his sleeve.

Robert looked down and quickly patted the sleeve, putting the fire out.

"Have you done this before?" the little boy asked.

"Oh, yes," Robert said. "I've slain many a dragon. I think. The key is not to give up."

Once more, Robert ran into the cave and was thrown out again.

And again.

And again. Every time he was thrown out, he became dirtier and more bruised.

That continued until finally a giant rock fell in front of the mouth of the cave. The dragon was trapped inside.

All the villagers looked up to see the little boy holding a large branch, which he had used as a lever to push the rock. The little boy gazed at the villagers, proud of his victory over the dragon.

Robert, who was very dirty and bruised, brushed himself off. He tried to cover his embarrassment.

"Yes," he said, looking at the little boy and his lever. "That works, too."

∼∽∼

In the front yard, Pip leaned over the edge of the well. "SOS!" he shouted. "We got a code red! Code black?

What's the bad one? That's what we got! You guys gettin' this? Andalasia? *Hello?*"

Meanwhile, inside the house, Giselle upended the box that usually held the Wand of Wishes, searching its contents for something useful. All she could find was a scroll.

"No one's answerin'!" Pip said.

Giselle turned to see Pip standing right next to her, and she let out a little yelp.

"You scared me to death!" Giselle said.

"Sorry," Pip said. "I'm stealthy now. Can't even hear *myself* comin'."

"Nancy said if I had any problems, I just had to ask . . ." Giselle started.

Then she took another look at the scroll and reached for it. But before she could grab the scroll, it jumped up and unfurled itself.

"Welcome to your magical wishing wand experience!" the scroll said brightly. "If ever you should have a question, just ask and I shall appear!"

Then—*poof!*—the scroll disappeared.

"Wait!" Giselle said.

"Where'd he go?" Pip asked as they looked all around.

"Hello?" Giselle said. "Mr. um . . . Scroll! Can we ask our question *now*?"

Poof! The scroll reappeared atop Pip the cat.

"Of course!" the scroll replied. "Ask any question and I shall appear!"

The scroll then slid off Pip.

"And just Scroll is fine. Mr. Scroll's my father. Although he was really more of a *booklet*—"

"We got no time for this!" Pip said, cutting off the scroll.

"Sorry. My friend's a little anxious, because we'd very much like to undo our wish as soon as possible," Giselle said, talking quickly.

"Didn't like what you got, huh?" the scroll asked. "Whadja wish for? Unicorns? Rainbows every day? Sounds great, right? Then the rain comes."

"Wasn't rainbows," Pip muttered under his breath.

"Actually, I, um . . . wished for a fairy-tale life, and it made my town into a place like Andalasia," Giselle said, her voice full of turmoil. "And now I'm slowly turning into a wicked stepmother."

"And I'm her soon-to-be-evil *cat*," Pip said desperately.

The scroll blinked. "Yes. That is definitely a wish to be unwished. Good luck!"

Then—*poof!*—the scroll disappeared again.

"Is he not pickin' up on the panic?" Pip said.

"What we need to know is *how* to unwish a wish?"

Giselle asked the air around her, hoping the scroll was still listening.

With another *poof!* the scroll reappeared on Giselle's shoulder and jumped off.

"No problem," the scroll said. "Let me check myself here."

The scroll glanced at himself, awkwardly reading upside down.

"Here it is! 'Wishing to unwish a wish.' Right. Okay. First we need to know how much of the real you is left. 'Cause you have to be *you* to unwish your wish! It's why we build in some time before a wish settles in. So let's see. Stepmothers are . . ."

The scroll pondered that for a moment, then said, "Well, they're *wicked*. We know that."

"Wicked *good*," Giselle said, her voice sounding perfectly evil.

She gasped, throwing her hand over her mouth. Wickedness was coursing through her again.

"Check on that one," the scroll said. "And if I'm remembering my villains right, the other three are vain, cruel, and ambitious."

Pip looked at Giselle and said, "I mean, she's definitely vain."

"I'm not vain," Giselle retorted. "I just look good in everything."

Once again, Giselle squeaked in horror.

"Right, so it's just those last two, and you'll be too evil to unwish your wish," the scroll noted. "Not to worry. As long as you unwish it before midnight, you'll be fine."

A scared look crossed Giselle's face.

"What happens at midnight?" she and Pip asked at the same time.

"On the stroke of twelve, the spell is set, and nothing will be as it was before," the scroll said. "It means your wish is permanent for all of time."

"Permanent?" Giselle said.

"For all of time? But there's so much fur in my mouth!" Pip moaned.

"Yep, so let's get to it," the scroll said. "To unwish your wish, all you have to do is take the wand labeled 'wand.'"

"For da love a' chestnuts, grab it!" Pip shouted.

"Yes!" a very nervous Giselle said. "It's right—"

But as Giselle turned to the side table where she had left the Wand of Wishes earlier, she was shocked to find that the magical object was *not* right there.

As terror welled up inside her, Giselle tore through all the garment bags, looking for the wand.

Pip anxiously glanced out the window, staring at the clock tower.

"Hurry!" he said. "It's almost—"

Dong!

The clock tower rang, and Giselle and Pip exchanged horrified looks. She rushed to the window only to see the clock strike two in the afternoon. At the stroke of noon, wickedness had coursed through her veins. When the one o'clock chime rang out, vanity had consumed her.

"Two o'clock," Giselle said with a gulp. "That means it's *cruelty*."

Then she looked down at Pip, steeling herself.

"No. We can't let it happen. Just don't give in to it," she said.

"I am not an evil cat. I am not an evil cat," Pip repeated to himself.

Dong!

The second chime rang out. Despite all her good intentions and best efforts, Giselle felt a shudder pass through her body. A dark look crossed her face as she slammed her hand down in front of the scroll.

"I am Giselle," she declared. "I am pure love, and you're going to do what *I* want."

Then Pip pounced on the scroll with devious intent. The scroll screamed and disappeared in a *poof!*

Pip tumbled past the spot where the scroll had been and fell off the couch.

Then, just as quickly as the cruel streak had come, it was gone.

"What did I do?" Giselle asked.

Pip popped up from the floor.

"You? Did I just murder somebody?" he asked as he looked at a tiny piece of paper on the floor. "Is that *him*?"

Filled with dread, Giselle gazed back at the clock tower.

"In one more hour I'll be a villain," Giselle said with fear in her voice. "You stay here. I have to find a way to stop this."

She ran off, leaving Pip behind. He watched her for a moment, until his attention drifted down to one of his paws.

"And I have ta lick this for some reason," Pip said, licking his paw and then gagging. "Yeah, that's *real* bad."

~ CHAPTER SIX ~

Morgan hurried down the street, looking for Tyson. At last, she saw him and his friends wandering into a market.

Summoning her courage, Morgan walked into the market. Merchants thronged the area, selling elixirs, potions, exotic-looking fruit, and just about anything else the imagination could conjure.

When Morgan sauntered over to a large display of dragon fruit, Tyson approached, trying to look every bit as casual as Morgan.

After an awkward moment of silence, Tyson picked up a dragon fruit, searching for something to say.

"This fruit is very squishy today," he said, squeezing the dragon fruit.

"I'd be careful, then," Morgan warned. "Squishy dragon fruit can be a bit—"

The dragon fruit cracked open, and a very small dragon burst out.

"Grumpy," Morgan finished.

Tyson dropped the fruit. He wiped his hands, trying to look cool.

"Well, I shall beware the squishy dragon fruit from now on," he said with a smile. "I assume you'll be attending the big festival this evening?"

"Oh, yes," Morgan said. "My stepmother doesn't normally allow such things—or anything, really—but this time she even bought me a new dress, and I intend to take full advantage of it."

"You're lucky," Tyson replied. "I wish *my* mother wouldn't allow it."

"You don't wish to go?" Morgan inquired. "Whyever not?"

"Well, for one, I have to dance with every princess in the land."

"Yes, that sounds like quite a chore," Morgan said with a smile.

Tyson smiled back. "I promise you it is," he insisted.

"Well, I'm sorry, but I don't believe that for a second," Morgan said.

To illustrate his point, Tyson began to sing about

how tiresome it was to dance with so many princesses when all he really wanted was to meet someone different.

Then he began to dance, and Morgan joined in, singing and dancing along with Tyson.

～～～

Giselle sprinted down the street, scanning the shops for anything that could possibly help her.

Just then, a small group of boys ran by, accidentally spraying Giselle's dress with mud. As if a switch had flipped, Giselle gave a cruel look to the boys.

She grabbed one of them by the arm. With fury in her voice, she said, "You little—"

But from deep within, the *real* Giselle fought back.

"Very sweet boy who's clearly done absolutely nothing wrong," the real Giselle said, back in control. "Run along now. Quickly, please."

She released the boy's arm, and he ran off. She was about to continue her search when across the street she saw Morgan and Tyson, smiling at each other.

"Oh, no," Giselle said, feeling the cruelty rising within her again. "No, no, no, no. Stepmothers never handle this well."

Morgan and Tyson walked toward her. Giselle turned away.

"So, will you save me a dance tonight?" Tyson asked. "Perhaps two?"

"Only if you dance like *that*," Morgan joked.

With an exaggerated bow, Tyson replied, "Whatever milady desires."

Morgan grinned at Tyson. Then they went their separate ways.

Giselle turned around.

Her face was a mask of cruelty as she smirked at her stepdaughter.

~~~

Rosaleen and Ruby scurried up the driveway to Malvina's house, fighting over the wand they had stolen from Giselle's home.

"I'll give it to her!" Rosaleen said.

"I'm the one who got it!" Ruby shot back.

"I'm the one who pulled you out!" Rosaleen noted.

"You wouldn't have been able to pull me out if *I* hadn't stolen it!" Ruby stated.

Rosaleen yanked the wand from Ruby, heading inside Malvina's home with Ruby right behind her.

Inside, they found Malvina standing in her throne room, consulting with Edgar. Rosaleen handed over the wand as they explained what had happened.

"So Giselle made some kind of a *wish* with it?" Edgar said, staring at the wand.

"That's what she said," Rosaleen offered.

"Then she turned her squirrel into a cat!" Ruby said, trying to top Rosaleen.

"Odd thing to do with a wish," Edgar thought aloud.

"Well, it *is* Giselle," Malvina said. Then she examined the Wand of Wishes. "Any wand of Giselle's can't possibly be very powerful, but I suppose we should see what I can do with it. Let's see. I wish . . . Ruby was a toad for all eternity."

Ruby squealed, squeezing her eyes shut tight. The wand's magic threw Malvina against the wall, causing her to drop the wand. Shelves tumbled around her. Rosaleen watched in horrified silence.

"Ribbit!" came from Ruby's throat. "Did it happen?"

Rosaleen slapped Ruby's arm; then Ruby opened her eyes. When she saw that she hadn't turned into a toad, she sighed with relief.

Malvina stood up and grabbed the wand.

"Mirror!" Malvina shrieked.

"Yes, Your Majesty," Edgar replied. "I'm asking every magic mirror I can find, Your Majesty."

Malvina stood there, anger oozing out of her pores. She glared at the wand.

"What kind of magic is *this*?" she asked.

Poof! The scroll suddenly appeared on the counter-top.

"Ask any question and I shall appear!" the scroll said cheerfully. "That's an easy one! It's Andalasian magic, which means only a true son or daughter of Andalasia can use . . . it. . . ."

The scroll slowed down as he began to realize that he was no longer in Giselle's possession. He saw the wand and then took a look at Malvina, Rosaleen, and Ruby.

"Oh," the scroll said. "Oh, no."

"Grab him!" Malvina ordered, and Rosaleen and Ruby took hold of him.

"What *is* it?" Rosaleen asked Ruby.

"He's so cute," Ruby squeaked.

"Please don't touch my fine print," the scroll begged.

"Did you say '*any* question'?" Malvina inquired.

The scroll attempted to pull away from Ruby and Rosaleen so he could disappear. It seemed as long as they were holding on, the scroll couldn't just *poof* away.

"Oh, no, you're not going anywhere," Malvina said with more than a trace of evil. "I have quite a few questions. So why don't you"—Malvina picked up a pair of scissors and leaned in—"start at the beginning."

The scroll gulped.

Morgan returned home, carrying a large basket full of wildflowers. She was humming a happy song as she daydreamed about the festival that evening.

She entered the house and went straight to her musty room in the attic. There she dropped the wildflowers on her cot and began sorting through them.

Morgan looked up when she heard Giselle enter the attic. "That's quite the bouquet," Giselle said in a cruel tone.

"Isn't it?" Morgan said. "They will match my dress perfectly, and I found them growing wild just near the market. Isn't that wonderful?"

"The world is truly a miracle," Giselle said. Now her voice was dripping with sarcasm. Of course it was, for Giselle was feeling particularly cruel.

"I must tell you," Morgan said, not picking up on the change in Giselle, "the most wonderful thing has happened. Tyson has asked me to the festival! Or I'm fairly certain he did. Well, we sang about it, which seems to suggest that. Either way, it's *wonderful*."

"Mmm, thrilling," Giselle said, clearly unimpressed. "But I'm afraid you won't be attending the festival tonight. You have way too many chores to do."

"But I've done all my chores," Morgan protested.

"Have you?" Giselle asked. "What about the carpet in the hall? Awfully dusty. And the windows? I can barely see a thing. And there's the gardening, and the sewing, and the mending, and don't forget the chimney. Filthy business."

"Okay," Morgan said. "Perhaps there are a few I missed, but surely they can wait."

Giselle glared at Morgan. "Are you speaking back to me?"

"Of course not," Morgan said, backing down. "I would never do such a thing."

"Perhaps you need to remember your place here," Giselle sneered. "Until you do, you are not to leave this room, except for chores. And *only* when I say."

Then a bag dropped from the ceiling, causing Morgan to jump back with a start. The bag contained the rag dress they had bought, as well as feather dusters and aprons. Morgan looked up and saw Pip the cat perched in a high corner. He rubbed his body against the corner, shedding all over it.

"Missed a spot," Pip said in a bratty tone.

"Yes, I can see there's much to do," Morgan said. "And I'll get to all of it right after the festival. I won't even sleep, but I promised Tyson I would be there."

"Oh, come now, Morgan," Giselle said. "A boy like that has plenty of options. And frankly, better ones. But don't worry. You can still enjoy the night up here from your little perch. I'm sure it will be just as magical."

Then a look of awareness crossed her face as Giselle said, "Oh! That was sarcasm, wasn't it? Huh. Not so hard to understand after all."

"Stepmother, please," Morgan begged. "Don't be this cruel."

"I can't help it, dear," Giselle said, relishing the moment. "It's just who I am."

Then Giselle revealed that she had been holding the Memory Tree and dropped it on top of the pile with the rag dress, the feather dusters, and the aprons. She turned away, slamming the door on her way out.

And Morgan?

Morgan could only stand there, crestfallen.

Then she heard the turn of a key.

The lock clicked into place.

Giselle had locked Morgan inside the attic.

And if she could have seen Giselle's face, Morgan would have witnessed a thin, cruel smile play across her wicked stepmother's lips.

⌇⌇⌇

Robert, looking and feeling considerably worse for the wear, hiked back toward the tavern. Upon his arrival, he saw the adventurers outside, getting on their horses, preparing to head for their homes.

"Prince Robert!" the warrior called out.

"How did we fare?" the grumpy prince asked.

Robert paused a moment, then said, "Well, there was a giant beast."

At that, the adventurers' eyes grew wide with excitement.

"And was there swordplay?" the warrior asked.

"There was . . . some. Yes," Robert said, thinking about what exactly constituted swordplay. "All in all, it was . . . fine. Maybe not 'heroic' in the classic sense. I'm not sure a day was saved, exactly."

That seemed to let the air out of the adventurers' collective balloon. They all exchanged knowing glances as they headed for their horses.

"Just walkin' through the woods," the grumpy prince said. "Over and over."

"And then ya die," the huntsman added.

"Perhaps tomorrow, though!" Robert offered.

"Keep telling yourself that," the warrior said, patting Robert on the back.

Then she got on her horse as Robert watched, refusing to give up on his quest for heroic adventure.

Meanwhile, in the attic, Morgan stood silently in her rag dress. She couldn't help staring at her sad reflection in the dusty mirror. She pulled up a strap and pinned it in place. But the strap fell back.

Sighing, she was about to give in to despair when she noticed something else in the mirror.

It was a dragon fruit from the market. She turned and went to pick it up. A smile danced across her lips as Morgan remembered her encounter with Tyson.

Slowly, an idea began to take root.

A few moments later, Morgan made a rope out of sheets. She tied one end inside her room, securing it tightly. Then she threw the rest out the attic window.

Peering down, Morgan took hold of the sheet and exited through the window, climbing down the wall. When she was only a few feet from the ground, she jumped, landing on her feet.

She was brushing off her rag dress when she heard someone say, "Going somewhere?"

Morgan turned around to see Giselle standing nearby, smirking.

"It's not what you think," Morgan said nervously. "I just have to tell him why I won't be there. Stepmother, please. I'll be back in no time at all."

"You're right," Giselle agreed. "You will. Because you're not going *anywhere*."

The cruel stepmother grabbed Morgan by the arm as Morgan whimpered, "Please. *Please* don't do this."

There was something about the sincerity in Morgan's voice that reached the real Giselle deep within, and for a moment, she remembered who she was.

"Morgan!" Giselle said, sounding horrified by herself.

"Stepmother?" Morgan asked.

Giselle shook her head, fighting off the cruelty within her, but it was a losing battle.

Then the town clock sounded the first of three chimes.

Dong!

"Oh, no!" Giselle gasped. "It can't be! Not yet!"

"What are you talking about?" Morgan asked, not understanding.

"Ambition," Giselle said. "It's the last one. Then I'm fully her."

"Fully who?"

But Giselle didn't answer. She looked around, desperation in her eyes. Then she saw the well behind them. She dragged Morgan to it.

"What's going on?" Morgan demanded.

"I'm sorry," Giselle said, just barely hanging on to her goodness. "It's all my fault! I wished that

Monroeville was like Andalasia, and it went terribly wrong—"

Dong! The second chime sounded. Morgan looked terrified.

"Or terribly right," Giselle said, her wicked alter ego back in charge. "Poor thing doesn't even know what she wants. But *I* do."

"Stepmother, please," Morgan said.

"You have to listen to me, okay?" Giselle said with tears in her eyes, trying to cling to her goodness as it slipped away.

"Oh, yes, yes, yes," Giselle's wicked alter ego answered. "Perfect little Morgan. Not so perfect now, is she?"

"Don't. You. Dare," Giselle threatened her inner evil foe.

"I'll dare all I like!"

"You're scaring me!" Morgan said, crying.

With all her might, the real Giselle pushed back through. "I know, and there's no time. I wish *I* could do it myself, but who knows what could happen if I went over there like this. *You* have to go. Get help before it's too late. And you only have until midnight to do it."

"*Do what?*" Morgan asked.

Dong!

The third chime rang out. Giselle gave Morgan one final loving look.

"Save us," Giselle said.

Then, without another word, she pushed Morgan into the well.

Morgan screamed as she fell. The good that was left in Giselle knew that Morgan wouldn't be hurt, that the well would take the girl safely to Andalasia.

But as Giselle shuddered one last time, whatever goodness was left in her was gone.

Now she was pure evil.

Giselle looked into the well. "Wretched girl," she said with sharp cruelty.

Then she glanced at the clock tower, no longer remotely concerned about what time it was.

The sound of crying came from within the house.

It was Sofia.

Giselle sighed, rolling her eyes.

"Who has time for that?" she said with distaste.

Then she saw three fairies nearby.

"You three look like you're good with children," Giselle said. "My precious darling needs tending to. See to that, won't you?"

It was clear to the fairies that it wasn't a request. It was a command.

And they obeyed.

~ CHAPTER SEVEN ~

Pip the cat admired himself in the mirror as he lounged, grooming himself. He alternated between using his sandpaper-like tongue and using the razor-sharp claws on his front paws.

Giselle strutted into their home with wicked vibes.

"I feel superior to all livin' things," Pip said. "Don't know why we were fightin' this."

Giselle looked at herself in the mirror with vanity. She primped, adjusting her hair.

"Indeed," she said. "Who knew being a villain could feel so *liberating*."

She smiled, reveling in the moment. But as she looked at her reflection in the mirror, she noticed something else. Something small, red, and sparkly.

Turning around, Giselle found a single ruby earring on the floor, and she picked it up.

She remembered seeing it *on* someone.

"You know, stepmothers may be many things," Giselle said, "but one thing they're not is *powerful*. It's why they have to go through all those ridiculous manipulations. They have no power of their own. Now that Morgan's gone, I'm not one anymore. So I think it's time I took on a new role in this town."

Then she looked at Pip and said, "I'd like to be *queen*."

"But ya already got a queen," Pip reminded her.

"That should be easy enough to fix," Giselle ambitiously proposed.

Pip smoothed down his pointed cat ears. "Where we goin'?" he asked.

"A villain like Malvina can never resist the chance to show the world how bad she is," Giselle said. "I say we give it to her, and then I have a little job for you, my pet."

"Ooh. Do I get to be evil now?" Pip asked.

"Oh, yes," Giselle replied as she continued to scheme.

~~~

Morgan blinked, again and again, as she slowly became aware of the two-dimensional world around

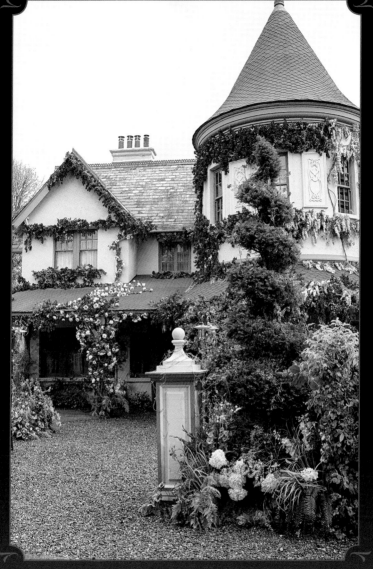

Giselle and her family move into a charming house in a small town called Monroeville.

In Morgan's new room, her old artwork is displayed, including her Memory Tree.

Malvina, Rosaleen, and Ruby stop by to greet Giselle and her family in their new home.

Malvina, Rosaleen, and Ruby host a bake sale for a big event called Monroe-Fest.

During her first day at her new school, Morgan meets Malvina's son, Tyson.

Giselle hosts her own bake sale. Morgan is embarrassed.

Morgan says Giselle will never be her real mother, only her stepmother.

Giselle uses the Wand of Wishes to wish that she and her family will have a fairy-tale life.

The wish comes true! Monroeville changes to Monrolasia, where everyone is in a fairy tale.

But Giselle realizes that as time passes, she is changing into a wicked stepmother!

Giselle visits Malvina, who has turned into an evil queen.

Giselle plans to take over Monrolasia.

Morgan uses her Memory Tree to turn Giselle back into her normal self.

her. She was groggy, confused, and baffled by the revolving vortex of light that hovered in the sky above her.

"Wh-what happ—" Morgan started.

But she stopped when she saw a fairy-tale butterfly flutter by, struggling to stay in the air.

"Huh?" Morgan said.

She sat up and wiggled her fingers. They looked flatter somehow.

Then her eyes widened as she saw a magnificent courtyard that had fallen into a state of ruin. There were cracks running along the old stone walls. The ivy that climbed the walls was dried up, the flowers dead. In the distance, Morgan saw a bridge that had crumbled into a pool.

Strangest of all were the little golden balls of light that drifted silently into the air toward the vortex, as if it was raining, only in reverse.

"Is this Andalasia?" Morgan wondered aloud.

A familiar voice came from behind her: "Morgan?"

Morgan recognized it immediately. It was Nancy's!

But as she turned around, Morgan was taken aback to see a different-looking Nancy and Edward, their swords raised. They were two-dimensional fairy-tale versions of themselves. And behind them was a host of fairy-tale creatures: a princess, a troll, a giant, an assortment of woodland animals, and, of course, a witch.

"What are you doing here?" Nancy asked.

"And why are you wearing a potato sack?" Edward asked, gesturing toward Morgan's dress.

∽∽∽

A little while later, Morgan sat in Nancy and Edward's castle, a blanket wrapped around her shoulders. The room they were sitting in was partially destroyed. The fairy-tale creatures were there as well, sitting around Morgan.

"And then I swept a chimney, and sang a song, and danced with a broom!" Morgan said, rambling. "And I didn't have one bad thought the whole time. Even when Giselle went crazy and pushed me down a well, I just said to myself, 'Wow! I'm falling down a well.' Then—*bam!*—I landed here, and now I'm me except . . . pointier."

Nancy gave the witch an inquisitive look.

"Is it possible coming here broke the spell?" Nancy asked the witch.

"A girl from the other world dropping here for the first time?" the witch said, thinking out loud. Then, with a shrug, she said, "Could happen. That process is very mysterious."

Nancy, Edward, and the magical creatures looked at Morgan, puzzled.

"At least we finally understand what's going on here," Nancy said.

Morgan looked around the dilapidated room. She saw more little balls of light drifting up into the air and disappearing into the vortex.

"What *is* going on here?" Morgan asked. "It's not exactly the fairyland I imagined."

"Last night our magic just started going somewhere," Edward explained.

The giant took a step forward.

"Giant can't lift," he said as he tried and failed to pick up the tiniest of chairs.

"And none of our animals can talk," the princess said.

As if on cue, a deer approached Morgan, but when it opened its mouth to speak, it coughed instead.

"And it's possible I'm a *teeny* bit less dashing today," Edward said, making it sound like the absolute end of the world. "It's tragic."

"Last night is when Giselle made her wish," Morgan said, the pieces of the puzzle coming together in her mind.

"Yes, and a wish as big as that wouldn't just need a *little* of our magic," the witch mused. "It would need *all* of it."

"And, Morgan, our land isn't designed to work without Andalasian magic," Nancy said. "It wouldn't be a good thing."

The words hit Morgan, and she said, "But *everything* here is made of magic. If it's all gone, what happens to Andalasia?"

No one said a word until, at last, the witch spoke.

"It will disappear forever," she said.

Morgan looked at all the magical creatures in the room. They seemed defeated as the little golden balls of light continued to vanish into the sky.

"I don't want Andalasia to disappear forever!" the giant said, crying uncontrollably.

A tiny fairy flew to the giant and placed a very small hand on his back to comfort him.

"Don't worry," the fairy said. "Their Majesties have a plan. Right, Your Majesties?"

All the creatures in the room turned their heads to look at Edward.

"Of course we do," Edward said with bravado. "It's a very good plan. Lots of bravery and saving of the day. Many songs will be sung of it!"

Then he looked at Nancy and whispered, "Quick, what's our very good plan?"

"We just have to do what we do best: make wishes come true," Nancy replied.

Then she turned to address the group.

"Andalasia, gather your magic," she said.

~~~

A little while later, the citizens of Andalasia had returned to the castle and were placing magical items into a massive pile. There were wands, vials, apples, spindles, mirrors, and more. Any object that contained even the slightest trace of magic was brought to the castle.

Little balls of light sailed up from the pile and headed for the growing vortex in the sky.

Morgan dug through the pile of magical items with Edward and Nancy, in search of something that might help them save the day.

Edward snatched up a beanstalk. He held it for the witch to see.

"Aha!" he said. "How 'bout this? Big magic. Very big. Legends have been sung about its—"

"Yes, it's very big magic," the witch said, cutting him off, "if you want to find a giant in the sky."

Edward tossed the beanstalk aside.

Then Morgan grabbed a teeny vial. "This?" she asked.

"Does Giselle need to be smaller?" the witch asked, confused.

A spindle caught Edward's eye, but then he thought better of it.

"Definitely not this one," he said, putting it aside.

Morgan stared at the pile of objects in frustration.

"Okay," she said, "we need something that can bring back our Giselle. What kind of magic is strong enough to make you remember what you forgot?"

Instantly, Nancy and Edward knew the answer.

"The Memory Tree!" they said in unison.

"She still has one?" Morgan asked, shocked.

"Of course," Edward said. "No Andalasian ever loses their Memory Tree. Even if they've lost themselves."

The swirling vortex above them caught Morgan's attention. She watched as it appeared to grow larger— angrier, even. All the magic from Andalasia was being sucked into it . . . and soon that magic would be gone.

"Hold on, Giselle," Morgan said.

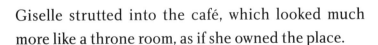

Giselle strutted into the café, which looked much more like a throne room, as if she owned the place.

There was a mad hatter attending what looked like a most interesting tea party while bakers filled tables with confections for the festival that evening. Among the treats were several pyramids made of mouth-watering cupcakes.

Malvina oversaw all the activity. She monitored everyone to make sure not one mistake was made. Meanwhile, Rosaleen and Ruby scurried around behind her, ensuring that Malvina's slightest whims were heeded.

Holding up a hand mirror, Malvina was just about to call for Edgar when she heard another voice instead.

"Mirror, mirror, in her hand . . ."

Malvina turned to see Giselle.

"Who's the most blatantly insecure woman, whose need to constantly ask her own reflection for validation suggests that what she really needs is to love *herself*, in all the land?" Giselle asked in a mocking tone.

Everyone stared at Malvina.

"Giselle, always a pleasure," Malvina said with insincerity.

"Yes," Giselle said. "I imagine it is. I was hoping I might run into you. And look at this! It seems I have."

The spectators sensed where all this was going (hint: nowhere good), and they promptly left the room.

"So what can I do for you, then?" Malvina asked. "As you can see, we're quite busy."

Giselle eyed the cupcakes. "Still with the baked goods," she said, practically tsk-tsking Malvina for her predictability. "This will only take a moment. I thought it only fair to give you a chance to hand Monrolasia over to me, *peacefully*, before any *unpleasantness* begins."

"And why would I do that?" Malvina asked.

"Because this town is mine," Giselle stated. "I think we both know that now."

Then she held up the ruby-red earring she had found in her home.

"Don't we?" she finished.

Malvina, Ruby, and Rosaleen stared at the earring. Ruby gasped.

But Malvina didn't seem to care. Or if she did, she didn't show it.

"I suppose we do," Malvina said. "But still, I must decline your *generous* offer. It's clear that Monrolasia is everything it was meant to be, however that might have occurred."

The two women stared at each other, neither conceding any ground to the other.

"Well, I tried," Giselle said. "If you won't accept my generous offer, there's only one way left to handle this."

"Indeed," Malvina agreed.

"One of us dies?" Giselle suggested.

"Say *midnight*?" Malvina said.

Then the clock in town struck six as the women looked at each other, satisfied with their agreement.

"That seems about right," Giselle said.

They exchanged icy glares, then left the shop in a hurry, pushing past each other. They both headed for home.

When Malvina arrived at her house, she went straight to her throne room, where she snatched up a cauldron and grabbed some malevolent-looking ingredients. She began to brew something awful.

After a while, she held up a dark vial that contained terrible smoking magic.

"I think we've got it," Malvina said.

She failed to notice Pip creeping out from behind a shadowy curtain.

Soon Robert returned home from a hard day of near-heroic adventure. He walked inside and found three fairies tending to Sofia. He gave them a curious look and then headed upstairs.

When he got to the bedroom, Robert saw Giselle admiring herself in a mirror with her back to him.

"Giselle, there you are!" Robert said, sounding tired. "I have had quite the day—"

Then Giselle whirled around, revealing a face that could only belong to an evil queen. Her eyes were accentuated with bold makeup, giving her a regal yet menacing air.

"That makes two of us," Giselle replied.

~~~

"I knew it was a tree house," Morgan said, taking it all in. "But that's a tree *house*."

"We do whimsy well here," Nancy said.

Then they entered the very tree house Giselle had once lived in. And even though its magic was fading, slowly being sucked up by the vortex, it still managed to appear dreamlike.

"It looks just like I imagined," Morgan said. She had heard the stories from Giselle since she was a little girl. Even the Prince Edward statue was there! The mannequin had two dazzling blue crystals for eyes and leaves for hair, and yet—curiously—it had no mouth.

Morgan watched as Edward looked at the statue.

"Hand me that comb," Edward said, sounding miffed.

Morgan gave him a comb, and Edward held it up to the mannequin's mouth.

But those lips were not to Edward's liking.

"Edward, can we maybe find your lips *after* we've saved our land from total and complete destruction?" Nancy asked politely.

Edward's actual lips moved into a pout. "Fine," he replied.

"Tree's over here," Nancy said as she opened a pane in a circular window.

Morgan and Edward followed her into the yard, in the middle of which sat Giselle's Memory Tree. The tree was covered in memory ornaments. Morgan saw pictures of her father, Sofia, and herself. They were all wonderful moments, frozen forever, reminders of the time they had spent together as a family.

The memories were intact, but the tree itself . . .

Morgan walked to it, feeling her heart break.

"It's dead," she said softly. "What do we do?"

"Never fear," Edward said, trying to sound brave. "We will come up with something very smart at the last minute that solves all our problems."

Nancy and Morgan stared at him.

"What? It's how it works here," he said.

"There has to be something we can do," Nancy said, thinking.

Maybe there was, but Morgan didn't know what. She looked at one of the ornaments on the Memory

Tree. It was a photo of her as a little girl, looking up at Giselle on top of a billboard. Morgan remembered that moment very well. It was the night she and her father had first met Giselle.

Morgan ran her finger over the image of her younger self. "That me would have figured it out. I spotted a magic princess on a crappy billboard in the rain from a taxicab! Probably why Giselle likes her better."

"Morgan, no, she doesn't," Nancy said.

"Yes, she does," Morgan continued. "And I get it. We never used to fight back then. We just had fun."

The warmth of the memory flooded through every fiber of her being.

"I know she thinks it's my fault that everything changed," Morgan said. "But the truth is . . . I miss it, too."

Without warning, the flowers that surrounded the ornaments began to glow. It lasted only a moment, but they glowed!

As the glow faded, Morgan said, "What was that?"

"Magic," Edward replied. Then a little ball of light rose from his hand toward the vortex. "Well, that's alarming," Edward added.

"Quick," Nancy said to Morgan, "look at another one."

Tentatively, Morgan did as Nancy said. In this memory, Morgan could see herself, again as a little girl, happily dancing with Giselle and her father in the living room of their New York City apartment. She remembered it like it was yesterday.

Again the flowers glowed, and again the glow faded.

"I can't!" Morgan said, frustrated. "I can't do it again."

Another ball of light drifted from Edward, this one from his chest. It sailed upward and into the vortex.

"Please," Edward begged. "Please try again."

"I don't know how," Morgan admitted.

Nancy walked over to Morgan and took her by the hand.

"Morgan, all you have to do is look inside," Nancy said.

And then Nancy began to sing of magic and how it was truly needed in that moment—not the kind of magic that came from spells or wands, but something from within Morgan.

Morgan tried again. The flowers began to light up once more.

"It's working!" she said, astonished.

She kept on looking at the memory ornaments, remembering all the wonderful times she and her family had shared over the years. There were birthday parties, first days of school, and soccer games. And wrapped up in each and every one of those memories was Giselle, and her love for her family.

Nancy continued singing as Morgan kept looking at the memories, and they grew, swirling all around them. Soon a portal began to form.

Magical energy from Edward, from all the animals around them, from everyone and everything in Andalasia continued to drift into the sky toward the vortex.

Meanwhile, the portal grew larger. It was now wide enough for them to enter.

Edward looked behind him, at all the creatures of Andalasia. He saw how terrified they were of losing their magic.

Nancy and Edward knew what had to be done.

Stepping away from Nancy and Morgan, Edward drew his sword and stood in front of his fellow Andalasians. On his honor, he would defend them to the very end.

Then, a moment later, with a loud *fwoosh*, Nancy and Morgan found themselves in Morgan's backyard in Monrolasia.

All around them, the magical glow of memories swirled and danced like ghosts. They watched as the magical trail shot around the side of Morgan's home and into the turret window.

The pair raced inside, and when they reached Morgan's room in the attic, Morgan saw a pile of clothes glowing with magic.

"What is that?" Nancy asked.

Morgan took a step closer. She saw that it wasn't the clothes glowing. It was something sitting on *top* of the clothes.

It was *her* Memory Tree!

The small pink tissue-paper flowers Morgan had glued onto it many years earlier now glowed with magic. In awe, Morgan picked up the Memory Tree.

"It's the power of love," Morgan said.

Maybe it wasn't too late, she thought. Maybe she could still save Giselle *and* Andalasia.

~ CHAPTER EIGHT ~

As the clock struck eleven-thirty at night, a carriage rolled down the road to downtown Monrolasia. Inside, Giselle sat with Robert as the horses trotted along.

"We're really going to need something more regal than this," Giselle said, gesturing with disgust around the carriage. "And minions. We'll need minions if we want anything done right."

"Where did you say Morgan was again?" Robert asked, a bit distracted.

"Oh, who knows?" Giselle said. "And who cares? This night is about *me*."

"Right," Robert said. "Stop the carriage," he said to the driver.

The driver obeyed, and the horses stopped. Robert hopped out of the carriage and into the crowd of people who were heading for the festival.

"Robert!" Giselle said, aghast at his behavior.

"Morgan wouldn't just disappear like that," Robert said. "If she did, something's wrong, and I'm going to find her."

"A fruitless quest," Giselle said dismissively. "But good luck with that."

Then, with a smirk, she turned to the driver.

"Drive," she commanded.

As the clock displayed 11:35, villagers were enjoying the fairy-tale party to end all fairy-tale parties. The streets were thronged with revelers enjoying themselves, eating delicious food and playing all kinds of carnival games. There was the True Love's Kissing Booth, the Witch's Brewing Station, and the Giant Turkey Leg Booth.

Everything was just as Malvina had wished it to be.

Even though the party raged in the streets, the ballroom was really where the fun was. Located inside the clock tower, the ballroom looked like a paradise. Flowering vines covered the walls from floor to ceiling. Chandeliers hung above the dancing crowd, illuminating their every move in the best possible light.

There was even an indoor waterfall. It streamed into an artificial moat that surrounded the dance floor. There the villagers moved to the rhythm of a stately waltz played by an orchestra.

Tyson was there, dancing with one princess after another. Each flirted with him, which he really did not enjoy.

In the center of it all was Malvina, seated on a throne and wearing her crown.

"Think I'll get some air," Tyson said to his mother. He hoped to escape the endless line of dancing princesses.

"Whatever, *dear*," Malvina said. "Back by midnight?"

He gave Malvina a curious look, then exited the ballroom.

Malvina looked down at the dark vial full of evil magic she had crafted in her cauldron. Her eyes flashed with deadly mischief.

∽∾∽

"It's so unfair," Rosaleen lamented.

She and Ruby stood in Malvina's house, staring at the Wand of Wishes, sparkling on the table. The scroll was there, too, tied up and trembling with fear.

A cheer erupted outside.

"I should be at that party," Rosaleen said to Ruby. "Instead, I'm babysitting you, babysitting this wand. All because she doesn't trust you."

Pip the cat stuck his head out from behind one of the curtains.

Lucky for Pip, the scroll was the only one who noticed.

Using incredible stealth, Pip got closer and closer to the wand.

"Or she doesn't trust *you*," Ruby jabbed.

Behind her, Pip clung to the back of a chair cast in shadows.

"I'm not the one she tried to turn into a toad," Rosaleen said.

"Maybe she likes toads," Ruby suggested.

Now closer, Pip balanced on a planter with remark-able grace.

"Please, no one likes a toad," Rosaleen claimed. "Clearly I'm her favorite, which means *you* should have to do the dumb stuff and *I* should be looking fabulous at that festival."

"Then *go*," Ruby said. "And I'll tell Malvina you abandoned the wand, and we'll see who ends up a toad." They continued to argue until finally Pip stood in front of the wand. He was about to take it with a paw when he heard someone say, "I wouldn't if I were you."

Pip looked up. Edgar stared at him from a mirror. Then Ruby and Rosaleen turned his way, too.

"Little advice from a cat . . ." Pip said to the women. "*Get a life.* She hates ya both."

Then he took the wand in his mouth and, with a slash of his claws, released the scroll.

As Rosaleen and Ruby chased after Pip, he contorted his body, easily avoiding their grasp.

"Mr. Cat, wait!" the scroll shouted.

Pip turned and saw the scroll following him at a slow pace.

(Well, slow by cat standards. By scroll standards, he was remarkably fast.)

"Wait for me," the scroll said, tripping over his folds. "My fine print is so annoying!"

"Roll yourself!" Pip mumbled, the wand clenched in his mouth. "Roll yourself up!"

The scroll jumped into the air and rolled himself up. Then Pip grabbed the scroll in his mouth and ran away with him and the wand.

～～～

The party was in full swing as Giselle's carriage pulled up to the festival's entrance. The wheels came to a halt when Pip appeared. He entered the carriage and dropped the wand and the scroll from his mouth.

"You're drooling so much! Look at me!" the scroll complained. "I'm all bloated. My bottom half is double its weight!"

"Tell me about it," Pip grumbled.

Giselle was pleased beyond measure. She took the wand, which was dripping with cat saliva.

Slightly disgusted, she used the scroll to wipe her hand. "Thank you, my pet," she said.

"Great, so now that you have the wand, you can fix your mistake," the scroll said. "Any more questions?"

In response, Giselle grinned wickedly.

"Absolutely not," she said as she exited the carriage. Then, before stepping into the shadows, Pip gave the scroll an equally wicked grin.

"Yeah, they're evil," the scroll said.

Morgan and Nancy quickly left the house and raced down the street, stopping for only the briefest of moments to catch their breath.

Clutching the Memory Tree in her hand, Morgan looked up at the clock. It was twenty minutes until midnight.

"Morgan!"

She turned to see Tyson riding toward her on horseback.

"Are you okay?" he asked, his voice full of concern.

"You have *no* idea," Morgan said. "Can you gimme a ride?"

"Of course," Tyson said, glad to be of assistance.

"Go!" Nancy said, looking at Morgan. "I'm right behind you."

Then Tyson helped Morgan onto the horse and they galloped off toward the festival.

Soon they arrived in the town square. Morgan spotted Giselle's carriage near the clock tower.

"Over there!" she said to Tyson as they pushed toward their destination.

The clock now read 11:45.

As Giselle entered the ballroom, she glared at the elaborate decorations, the dancing partygoers, and especially Malvina, perched on her throne with the crown resting on her head, looking like she was above it all.

"Never met a throne she didn't like," Giselle said with snark.

She walked behind a giant chocolate sculpture of

Malvina. She glanced at the wand in her hand. A devious gleam flickered in her eyes.

"Now, let's see," Giselle said. "I wish . . ."

Then she closed her eyes and a moment later continued: "To be *queen* of Monrolasia."

Opening her eyes, she added, "*Evil* queen. Wording is everything with these things."

The Wand of Wishes sparkled, and then—*fwoosh!*—Malvina's crown appeared on Giselle's head.

Malvina, unaware of Giselle's actions, grabbed her head, reaching for the crown, which was no longer there.

Suddenly, the music stopped playing. The dancing stopped.

The whole room went silent.

"Why did you stop?" Malvina asked, perplexed.

"Because I *wished* it," Giselle explained as she walked over, wand in hand.

That was when Malvina recognized the crown Giselle wore.

It was *her* crown. She quickly put the pieces together.

"Can't trust those two with anything," she said, thinking about Rosaleen and Ruby. "Guess we'll have to settle this queen to queen?"

"It appears so," Giselle agreed.

They stared at each other, savoring the sinister, malicious moment.

Then they flicked their wrists at each other. The action sent them flying back in opposite directions. Malvina flew over the top of her throne.

Giselle slammed right into the orchestra with a loud crash. She got back on her feet quickly, grabbed her wand, and held it aloft. Only it wasn't a wand—it was the conductor's baton! Giselle tossed the baton to the cowering conductor. Then she picked up her wand from the floor.

"Play on," she instructed. The conductor was too terrified to do anything but comply.

Then the ground began to shake and a chandelier started to sway.

Giselle smirked, eagerly awaiting the havoc that was about to be wreaked.

Outside, the shaking ground knocked villagers off balance. Morgan held on to Tyson's arm to avoid falling over.

"What was that?" Tyson asked.

Morgan looked up at the clock tower and saw the time.

It was 11:50.

"Andalasia," Morgan said, making sure she still had the Memory Tree. "It's coming."

Then came a loud crash. Morgan and Tyson tumbled backward. Twisted tree limbs broke through the pavement, and a shimmering golden light shot through the cracks.

The crowd screamed.

〜〜〜

Robert approached a stream of people fleeing from the town square in terror.

The ground shook beneath his feet, nearly knocking him down. Then Robert saw a familiar face: it was Nancy! She was pushing against the crowd, heading directly toward whatever everyone else was running from.

"Nancy!" he shouted, rushing to her side. "Have you seen Morgan?"

"Yeah, she's fine," Nancy said. "But we have to get to the square. Giselle—"

"Something's wrong, I know," Robert interrupted. "I think we're going to need some help."

〜〜〜

Malvina glanced up in mid-fight at the chandelier above Giselle and had a horrible idea. She waved her hand, and magically, the chandelier fell.

Giselle zapped it with her wand before it could crush her, turning the chandelier into a flock of bluebirds.

But not just any bluebirds.

These were *furious* bluebirds.

They swooped down on Malvina.

"Weapons," Malvina commanded without missing a beat.

At once, an assortment of maces, whips, sledgehammers, and more popped into the hands of the festivalgoers.

"Destroy her!" Malvina shouted with a flick of her wrist.

Under Malvina's control, the festivalgoers headed for Giselle.

"Oh, Malvina," Giselle said, "love is stronger than hate."

With a zap of her wand, Giselle changed the weapons in the hands of the festival attendees to butterflies.

As their battle raged, the walls of the ballroom crumbled. Tree branches crashed through from the outside, tearing a huge hole in the wall.

Free of Malvina's control, the festivalgoers ran through the hole, seizing the opportunity to escape.

Crash! Malvina smashed into a mirrored wall.

"Guess you're not the fairest of them all," Giselle gloated. Once again, Malvina flicked her hand, causing the floor beneath Giselle's feet to give way. Giselle fell through the floor.

"Neither are you, dear," Malvina said.

〜〜〜

Outside on the street, the festival had devolved into chaos. More and more pieces of Andalasia were traveling through the vortex now, appearing in Monrolasia. Animals from Andalasia had crossed over into the real world and were stampeding through the streets, scared and alarmed. The world of Andalasia was merging with Monrolasia. Who knew what would become of either?

Morgan watched as the clock hit 11:53. Twisted branches and vines snaked their way around the outside of the clock tower. They knitted themselves together, creating a nearly impenetrable wall.

Despite the seeming impossibility of it, Morgan and Tyson had to get inside. Their loved ones were in the ballroom; they had to do whatever they could to save them.

Tyson attempted to slash his way through the vines while Morgan tried to pull them off the clock tower. But the vines were growing far too rapidly now. The vegetation on the wall thickened despite their best efforts.

"Morgan!"

Morgan spun around and saw her father rushing through the crowd. Robert threw his arms around his daughter, tightly hugging her.

"You're okay," he said as Nancy arrived.

"I am," Morgan said. "But Giselle—"

"I know," Robert said. "I came to help, and I brought some friends."

"We only have a few minutes," Morgan replied, checking for the Memory Tree as she looked at the clock with desperation. "I *have* to get inside!"

That was when Morgan saw them: a band of adventurers standing behind Robert. They all looked as if they had been waiting for that moment for years. They exuded bravery, and it was contagious.

"It's time to be heroes," Robert said.

At that, the adventurers drew their swords and began to hack and slash away at the branches and vines. They grabbed at the branches, pulling them away, making just enough room for Morgan to squeeze through.

A moment later, Morgan found herself inside the ballroom, followed by Tyson, Nancy, and Robert. She was shocked at what she saw. It looked like a strange hybrid world—a combination of Monrolasia and Andalasia. It was half ballroom, half forest, with bright grass and trees coming in from the walls.

In the middle of it all, a battle raged. The villagers who remained sparred as Giselle and Malvina continued their fight. Their fury was at its peak. Neither would give so much as an inch.

Simultaneously, Giselle and Malvina raised their hands and began to magically choke each other.

"This town's only big enough . . ." Malvina gasped.

"For *me*," Giselle gulped, her throat constricted.

Then Giselle squeezed Malvina harder and raised her into the air. Malvina tried to hold her magical grasp on Giselle, but she was slipping.

The time was now 11:55. In just five short minutes, the change would be complete, and Giselle would be evil forever.

Morgan dodged swords, ducking behind turned-over tables, rocks, and whatever else she had to as she made her way toward Giselle.

She was getting closer when she was knocked to the ground. The blow caused her to drop the Memory Tree she had clutched in her hands. It flew right into the massive fight, where it was instantly shredded.

"Nooooooo!" Morgan wailed.

Her only hope vanished.

But then something happened. The tiny shreds of her Memory Tree did not fall.

Instead, they began to swirl around, bathed in a last bit of Andalasian magic holding out against the darkness. It was subtle at first, but the swirling slowly took on a life of its own. The bits of paper whipped around Giselle, forming a maelstrom of memories, as all the love, all the emotions the family had felt for years enveloped her.

Then there was an explosion of light. Giselle released Malvina.

Malvina hit the ground, letting go of Giselle, who fell to the floor as well.

The crown tumbled off Giselle's head.

The room was silent.

Then Giselle looked up as Morgan watched her from across the room.

"Morgan?" Giselle said, her gentle voice overflowing with relief.

The kindness returned to her eyes.

The real Giselle was back.

Nancy rushed to Giselle.

"Where's Edward?" Giselle asked Nancy.

"He doesn't have much time," Nancy replied.

In the waterfall, Giselle saw a reflection of

Andalasia crumbling. Without any time to spare, she grabbed the Wand of Wishes.

She was just about to make her wish when a voice commanded, "Stop."

Giselle turned and saw Malvina.

"I wouldn't if I were you," Malvina warned.

Stepping aside, Malvina revealed Morgan. She was asleep, surrounded by a sparkly dark mist. Her body was suspended by vines wrapped around her.

"Morgan!" Giselle and Robert shouted.

Malvina held an open vial in her hand and put the stopper back in.

"What did you do?" Giselle gasped.

"Relax," Malvina said. "It's just a little sleeping potion. It was actually meant for you, but this'll do."

"Malvina, you have to undo it," Giselle pleaded.

"We'll see," Malvina said. "Your helpful scroll explained that come midnight, your wish is permanent. And I like this world. So you're going to drop that wand and let the clock strike."

"But if I do that, Andalasia dies," Giselle replied.

"And if you don't do it, *she* dies," Malvina said, gesturing toward Morgan. Then she subtly squeezed her hand into a fist.

Giselle watched in horror as the vines wrapped

around Morgan even tighter. The teenager wheezed in her slumber.

"Cease, evil witch!" Robert ordered.

He and Nancy rushed Malvina, but the evil queen used her magic to push them away.

Morgan's skin began to turn blue as the vines continued to constrict around her.

"Malvina, *stop!*" Giselle begged. "*Please!* This isn't you."

"It is now," Malvina said. "Just as you"—the evil queen squeezed her fist tighter—"wished it."

With that, the last of the air in Morgan's lungs was forced out.

Giselle dropped the wand. As it hit the floor, Morgan's eyes snapped open. The vines wriggled away, and the color of life returned to the teenager's cheeks.

Dong! The clock struck midnight.

The magic slowly began to flow away from Giselle.

~ CHAPTER NINE ~

In the waterfall, Nancy could see exactly what was happening at that moment in Andalasia.

There was Edward, falling to his knees, the magical glow draining from his body.

Behind her in the ballroom, Pip, still in cat form, tumbled out of the shadows. The same magical glow drained from his body and sunk into the ground.

The magic continued to flow away from Giselle, too. She grew weaker.

Malvina stepped forward.

Crack!

The broken Wand of Wishes was beneath her foot.

The second chime rang out from the clock. Malvina found her crown on the floor and placed it back on her head.

Dong!

Outside the ballroom, the buildings that lined the street began to get dark, one by one.

The sign that had welcomed everyone to the land of Monrolasia had changed as well. It now read WELCOME TO MONROLASIA—YOUR FAIRY TALE ENDS HERE.

The clock chimed again.

Inside the ballroom an explosion shattered the floorboards. The villagers who remained leapt out of the way as smoke and debris filled the room.

When it cleared, Giselle's tree house from Andalasia appeared against the back wall. It was nearly destroyed.

At the foot of the tree house was Morgan, holding Giselle, who was growing weaker with each breath. The magic within her was nearly gone.

The clock chimed once more.

Robert looked at his daughter and his wife.

"No!" he shouted. "This is *not* how this ends!"

He ran out of the ballroom.

"Some *hero*," Malvina said with a smirk.

Morgan barely heard the sixth clock chime as she clasped her mother's hand.

"Please hold on, please hold on," she begged.

On the floor, Giselle could barely keep her eyes open. She looked at her daughter. Then she saw her tree house. It was broken, just like the world she had made.

"I'm so sorry," Giselle said as her eyes started to close.

"I let you down," Morgan cried as the seventh chime rang out.

"Oh, Morgan," Giselle said as the life within her began to fade, "you could *never* let me down. *I* did this. Not you."

Another chime, and Morgan cried even harder. Giselle had very little time.

"Please," she begged. "*Please.* What do we do?"

"There's not much we can do, my love," Giselle answered.

Another chime sounded as the wind howled.

Soon Giselle's wish would be permanent and Andalasia would be lost forever.

"I know it's scary," Giselle said, struggling to speak. "But you'll be okay. You're strong, and you know who you are, no matter what world you're in. I've never worried about what you'll become."

Morgan watched the light in Giselle's eyes fade further.

"I just wish . . ." Giselle said, her voice trailing off.

The clock chimed again.

Giselle's eyes drifted from Morgan toward the

broken pieces of wand, only a few feet away. They seemed to sparkle, as if calling to Giselle.

The life came back to Giselle's eyes.

"What is it?" Morgan asked.

"That piece of wand," Giselle said. *"Grab it."*

Dong!

There was only one chime left.

Malvina smiled as she, too, heard the eleventh chime, her reign of wrath about to be cemented for all time. She was in all her glory, relishing her victory. She waved her hand and—*fwoosh!*—both Ruby and Rosaleen appeared before her, transported from Malvina's house.

"Your Majesty," Rosaleen said, "this was *her* fault—"

The words were meaningless to Malvina. She used her magic to transform her two minions into toads at last.

"Now you can *both* lick my boots," Malvina said with a cackle.

When Robert left the ballroom, he had gone straight to the clock tower. He sprinted up the spiral staircase, heading for the clockwork.

Arriving at the top, he saw the gears, ropes, and

pulleys that enabled the clock to move. Thinking fast, he drew his sword just as the last bell was about to ring.

Then he slammed the sword into the gears. The clock stopped.

The final chime did not ring out.

Malvina looked up, furious. She had been expecting the final chime, but now there was silence.

Morgan realized there was still time. She returned to Giselle's side with the pieces of broken wand in her hand.

"I got it," Morgan said. "But it's broken."

"S'okay," Giselle said weakly. "We have to make a *new* wish."

Then Giselle's eyes fluttered closed.

Morgan shook her. "Here," she said.

She tried to place the wand pieces in Giselle's hand, but Giselle didn't have the strength to hold them.

"I think *you* have to do it," Giselle gasped.

"But I can't use it," Morgan said. "I'm not a true daughter of Andalasia."

"You *are* a true daughter of Andalasia," Giselle said weakly. "Because you are *my* daughter, Morgan."

And then, with every ounce of strength she had left

within her, Giselle sang softly and sweetly to Morgan about how proud she was of her and how the love she had for Morgan would always be with her.

Giselle didn't get a chance to finish her song.

She was too weak. Her eyes fluttered closed.

A wave of panic and heartbreak overcame Morgan.

"Wait. What do I wish for? What do I wish for!" she said desperately.

But Giselle didn't reply.

Morgan took a deep breath and cleared her mind.

"Just look inside," she said to herself. "Look inside."

As she looked down at the pieces of the wand, Malvina glared at her.

Malvina realized what Morgan was about to do. She summoned her dark magic, waving her hand at the tower. With an earsplitting crash, the glass blew out.

Inside the tower, Robert shielded himself from the shards of glass that flew around him. With tremendous effort, he tried to hold the sword steady. But his fingers slipped, and the gears of the clock began to slide.

Back in the ballroom, Morgan looked up at Giselle's tree house, remembering what it was like being there. With stunning clarity, Morgan knew exactly what to do. She looked at the pieces of the wand in her hand.

"Don't you *dare*," Malvina said menacingly. She

raised her hands, ready to blast Morgan with her magic.

The gears of the clock resumed their grind. Finally, the last chime rang out.

Morgan closed her eyes tightly as she said, "I wish I was home with my mom."

All at once, there was a brilliant flash of light.

Malvina screamed.

Robert struggled in the tower while Nancy helplessly watched the weakening Edward's reflection in the waterfall.

Pip the cat held the scroll's hand.

Giselle's very last breath ebbed away.

~ CHAPTER TEN ~

Giselle's eyes opened.

It was morning in her quiet bedroom. She sat right up in bed. Her room was warm, and the sun came through the window. It looked like a plain old regular sun.

Not a fairy-tale sun.

Giselle wondered: could it be?

She ran downstairs to the kitchen. None of the appliances were singing.

Whew.

She heard Robert say, "Morning," as he entered the kitchen with a smile, holding Sofia in his arms. Robert kissed his baby daughter.

Then Giselle ran to him and hugged him.

"You're okay!" Giselle shouted.

"Uh, yeah," Robert said. "Had some crazy dreams, though."

"Dreams?" Giselle said. Then she remembered. "Andalasia!"

She rushed out the door, into the yard, and to the well. Looking inside, she saw that Andalasia was restored to its former self. Edward and Nancy were standing on the balcony of their castle, waving.

Pip was there, too. He was no longer a cat, but a chipmunk once more. He squeaked happily, bouncing up and down.

The scroll was there, too, and he gave Giselle a thumbs-up.

She sighed in relief as Robert walked over to her.

"You okay?" he asked.

"Oh, yes," Giselle said. "I'm fine now. But there's something I have to tell you."

"Ah, me too," Robert said. "I've been thinking about what happened yesterday and what you asked me, and I think it might be time for a change."

"What do you mean?"

"Well, I went for a walk this morning and I realized a small town like this could use a lawyer like me," Robert said. "Not just for divorces, but for everything. Maybe I could even do some good."

"But isn't that *less* exciting?" Giselle asked.

Robert shrugged. "Exciting is overrated. I think what I'm looking for is right *here*."

Giselle was so happy she threw her arms around Robert, and they kissed. It was a magical kiss. In fact, one might say that it was true love's kiss—and one would be right.

"Mom?"

Giselle turned to see Morgan rushing toward her.

"You did it!" Giselle said with pride.

"I was so scared," Morgan said. "I didn't know if it was going to work!"

"Okay, I missed something," Robert said.

Giselle and Morgan grinned at each other.

"I was about to explain . . ." Giselle started.

"Why don't you tell me over breakfast?" Robert suggested. "Oven's still not working, so I say we go out and celebrate."

"Celebrate what?" Morgan asked.

Robert paused for a moment, then said, "A fresh start."

He smiled and went inside the house.

"He doesn't remember any of it?" Morgan asked.

"Only the person who wields magic ever remembers it clearly," Giselle said. "For everyone else, it's more like a dream. Or I guess a nightmare in our case. Anyway, we'll fill him in later. Pancakes will help."

Morgan smiled.

"And after that, I think you and *I* should celebrate defeating an evil queen, with the non-world-killing 'magic' of credit cards," Morgan said.

Giselle felt a flush of warmth as she remembered the moment years earlier when a young Morgan had explained to her the "magic of credit cards."

"I'd love to," Giselle said, "but there's one thing I have to do first."

A little while later, Giselle walked through the door of Edgar's café. Edgar himself was staring into a mirror behind the coffee bar with a weird look on his face. It was as if there was something about the mirror he could almost remember.

"Morning, Edgar!" Giselle said.

He startled, then turned to Giselle and smiled.

"Giselle," Edgar said, focusing himself. "The usual?"

"Yes, thank you, Edgar," Giselle said. "Is Malvina around?"

"Where she always is," Edgar noted.

Giselle saw Malvina quietly sitting in her throne-like chair. Ruby and Rosaleen were there, as usual, on either side. They all held steaming cups of coffee and stared blankly ahead, not drinking.

"I hate bake sales," Ruby blurted out.

"And toads," Rosaleen said. "I had a horrible dream about toads."

"Me too!" Ruby said. "Were yours at a bake sale?"

Malvina saw Giselle walking toward her. She straightened up.

"Sorry to interrupt," Giselle said. "Just thought I'd say hi, and, um . . ."

Then Giselle leaned in and said softly to Malvina, "I wanted to apologize for the cupcakes yesterday. Actually, for a lot of things. I just really wanted Morgan to be happy here, and I got a little carried away."

Malvina looked at Giselle for a moment.

"Okay, well, enjoy your coffee," Giselle finished.

She was turning to leave when Malvina said, "You know, I have the tendency to get carried away myself, *sometimes.*"

Giselle smiled.

"It turns out we actually do have room on one of our committees, if you're interested," Malvina said. "I think our town could really use someone like you."

For a brief moment, it was almost like Malvina remembered what had happened. But perhaps that was just Giselle's imagination.

"I'd love that," Giselle said.

~ EPILOGUE ~

"So, we reach the end of our story," Pip said as he turned the very last page of the book.

Nip and Kip were almost asleep.

Pip explained that everything had returned to normal in Monroeville, except it was like everyone somehow knew that something had changed, too.

He told his children about a conversation Morgan and Tyson had after the whole Wand of Wishes incident.

It happened in the schoolyard.

"So, um, my friends and I are heading to Monroe-Fest later," Tyson said. "I know it's kind of boring, but there's not really much else to do in this town, so if you wanna join us, I could ... escort you."

" 'Escort' me?" Morgan asked.

"Yeah, I don't know where that just came from," Tyson admitted.

Morgan smiled and said, "Um, sure. Sounds like just the right amount of boring for me."

"Great," Tyson replied. "I'll pick you up."

He smiled at Morgan and then headed into the crowd as Morgan watched dreamily.

Maybe this new place will be wonderful after all, she thought.

Pip told his children about Robert, too, and how he opened up his small lawyer business in Monroeville. He was looking forward to helping his fellow citizens.

And next door to Robert's office, Giselle opened her own shop, called A Fairy-Tale Life. She went there every day, with Sofia in the stroller and Robert right next door.

Before they drifted off to sleep, Kip and Nip wanted to know what happened to Morgan's bedroom.

Pip told them that it was finally finished and no longer an electrical nightmare. It was more modern and less fairy-tale. It made Morgan happy.

But the thing Morgan loved best about her room in the new home was the Memory Tree that hung on her wall. It might have looked a little dingy, but it meant the world to Morgan.

One day, Morgan noticed that Giselle had come home from work and stood in her doorway teary-eyed.

"Mom," Morgan said with a hint of an eye roll.

"I'm sorry," Giselle said, wiping the tears away. "It just looks very nice there."

Morgan shook her head and sighed.

Then a loud noise came from outside: the sound of the well.

"Our dinner guests are here," Morgan said. She walked past Giselle, who gave her a kiss on the cheek.

Morgan chuckled.

In the backyard, Morgan, Giselle, and Robert, holding Sofia, greeted Nancy and Edward.

They had a new tradition: Sunday dinner together.

The couple had brought a gift as well, and they handed it to Giselle. It was a golden platter.

"Any dish you shall wish will appear on this plate," Edward said. "That's all it does. We're fairly certain . . . You know what? Why don't we just make the wish," Edward suggested as he took the platter back.

"Good idea," Morgan said.

They all laughed as they headed inside the house.

Before she went in, Giselle took a moment to reflect on all the joy and wonder in her life and how much she loved her family. There might be good days and bad days, but they would always have each other, making new enchanted memories together.

With those last words, Pip looked up from his book and saw that finally Nip and Kip were fast asleep.

He looked at his children and then at the last page in his book, which read simply . . .

THE END.